CHRONICLES OF V

Glass Stars

TASCHE LAINE

Cover Design by 100 Covers, 100covers.com

ISBN-13: 978-1-732-12615-2 (ebook)

ISBN-13: 978-1-732-12616-9 (paperback)

ISBN-13: 978-1-955674-11-9 (hardcover)

Library of Congress Control Number: 2021915588

Printed in the United States of America

Third Edition 2022

Skye Blue Press

Vancouver, WA

https://skyebluepress.com

CONTENTS

In Loving Memory of
Charmel Ulrich
July 8, 1966-August 10, 1980.
A beautiful, vibrant life taken much too soon.

"Death leaves a heartache no one can heal, love leaves a memory no one can steal."

— UNKNOWN

SIERRA HIGH SCHOOL

I

FIRST-DAY JITTERS

I raced through the hallways of Sierra High School, determined to find Emma before the bell rang. Just as I rounded the corner, a deep, booming voice stopped me in my tracks.

"Hold on there, Miss Jiménez. Where are you going in such a hurry?"

I spun around to see the principal walking toward me, a stern look on his face. His grizzled beard and gray suit made him an imposing figure.

Great. What a way to start my first day of high school. I'm in trouble already, I thought.

"Good morning, Violet," Dr. Michael Fitzgibbon said, all smiles by the time he reached me. "How are you today? Did you have a nice summer?"

"Yes, sir—wait." I scratched my head. "I'm not in trouble for running in the halls?"

"Nah, I just had to yell at you for appearances," he said. "You know, to keep up the mean principal façade—at least for the first week." He winked at me, but it looked more like something got stuck in his eye. He cleared his throat and added, "How are your parents? Ready for another stellar year, no doubt."

"Yes, I guess so." I looked at my feet, eager for this conversation to end so I could find Emma.

Dr. Fitzgibbon (or Fitz, but we didn't call him that to his face) furrowed his brow. He leaned down and spoke in a low voice, concern etched in his face. "Violet, is everything all right? You were in a big hurry just now. And first period doesn't begin for another fifteen minutes."

"Yes, sir, I'm fine. I'm just looking for my friend, that's all. And . . . I'm a little nervous," I admitted.

"There's no reason to be nervous, Violet. Just because your parents are rock stars at this school, it's not like you live in their shadow, right?"

"Right," I said and tried to smile. *Just what I need, the principal wants to be my new BFF because my parents are teachers here. Like that's not bad enough.*

"Sorry, that was supposed to be a lame joke. What I meant to say is everyone loves your parents. And I'm sure they'll love you, too. Just relax and be your awesome self. Have a good day, but slow down a bit, okay?"

"Okay, I will. Thank you, sir. Um, bye." I walked away from Dr. Fitz as fast as my legs would carry me—without running.

Now, where the heck is Emma?

EARLIER THAT MORNING, Emma and I made plans to wear our matching Taylor Swift *1989* T-shirts to our first day of high school. I wasn't a big Taylor Swift fan, but Emma was, and I'd do anything to make my best friend happy.

Well, if I'm being honest, Emma was my only friend. We did everything together. So when she wanted to go to Taylor Swift's *1989* concert a few weeks ago, I went. Emma called herself a Swiftie and knew every line from every song, which could be annoying when she randomly belted out lyrics at inappropriate times.

Emma had sent me an excited text before I'd even finished getting ready.

EMMA

I'm so psyched for the first freaking day of high school!!! Aren't u?

Psyched is not the word that comes to mind. Now stop texting me and let me finish getting ready!

OK sorry. See you in a few!

I was about to reply when my mom called me from downstairs. I shoved my phone into the back pocket of my ripped jeans and dashed out of my room.

"Good morning, Violet," Mom said and smiled at me when I walked into the kitchen.

I cringed.

"Do you want eggs for breakfast?" she asked, loud and cheery.

"Mom! How many times do I have to tell you? It's V! Call me V. Geez."

"Sorry, sweetie. I guess I need to be reminded a few more times." Mom cleared her throat and emphasized, "V, do you want eggs and—?"

"No, I'll just grab a banana." I looked at the empty spot on the counter where Mom usually kept the fruit. "Um . . . where are the bananas?"

"Good morning, sunshine," Dad said. He smirked and tousled my stringy hair as he handed me a banana from the bowl of fruit directly in front of me at the kitchen island. He combed his fingers through his own shaggy, black locks and asked with a wink, "Get enough sleep last night, V? Or are you nervous about your first day of high school?"

"You know I'm not a morning person, Dad." I grabbed the banana and plopped down on the bar stool with a loud thump. I pulled the banana peel down with hostility, bit off the top, and glared at my family.

"Grouchy bear! Grouchy bear! V is a grouchy bear!" Scotty, my six-year-old brother, sang out with a mouthful of scrambled egg. He looked like a mini troll doll with blond hair and big blue eyes.

My mom had thick, medium-length red hair that cascaded down around her face and shoulders like an unruly lion's mane. My dad had dark hair, eyes, and skin. My auburn hair was stick-straight and hung limply to the middle of my back. I couldn't do a thing with it. So how did Scotty end up with platinum blond hair? Easy—he was adopted.

"Shut up, brat!"

"Hey, don't tell your brother to shut up," Dad scolded. "He's just having a little fun with you. Besides, it's true. You could try to be civil. It's a big first day for him, too."

"Sorry," I grumbled.

"That's okay. I forgive you," Scotty said. "I'm starting first grade today! I forgive everyone."

My parents chuckled. "Sweetheart, what do you think 'forgive' means?" Mom asked.

"It means to be nice. I'm nice to V, and I'll be nice to everybody at school today, so I can make lots and lots of new friends."

"How precious is that? V, you should 'forgive' everyone today, like Scotty." Mom's fern-green eyes danced with mischief.

"Cute. Real cute." I shot her an icy stare with my bright green cat-like eyes and walked out of the kitchen to get my backpack.

WALKING into school with my parents that morning was the equivalent of the classic nightmare where you're naked and everyone's staring at you. Being a freshman on the first day in a new school was bad enough. And being a freshman whose parents taught at the *same* school? *Priceless.*

"Have a wonderful day, V," my mother gushed.

"Got a hug for your old dad?" Dad's lanky outstretched arms waited to wrap me up in them. At six-foot-five, he'd be intimidating if he weren't so thin.

I dodged the hug, backed away, and said, "No time. Gotta find Emma. Have a good day, you two. See ya later."

Dad pushed his hair back off his face and waved.

2

MORNING LIKE MOLASSES

I couldn't find Emma anywhere. I practically searched the entire school. And worse, she wasn't answering any of my texts. She always answered my texts. She always had her phone with her. It was a part of her, like an extension of her hand.

By the time the bell rang for first period, I had soothed myself by thinking Emma's phone must have died. Or maybe she'd forgotten it at home and went back to get it—that would be so like her. She wouldn't dare show up to the first day of school without her precious phone.

She'll show any minute. I'm sure of it.

The tardy bell rang. I took a seat in the third row and stared at the door. First period was Honors English 9. We'd picked up our schedules yesterday and only had one class together —this one.

So where is she? I don't get it.

She'd been so excited for high school to start. She kept saying how it would be better than junior high and how she couldn't wait for more freedom. She'd gone on and on about how she looked forward to being treated like an adult, not a kid —all summer. It was practically all she'd talked about. There's no way she'd miss the first day.

"Violet?" I heard a voice in the back of my mind, but it didn't register. "Violet? Are you all right?"

Suddenly, all eyes were on me. I shrank down in my seat and muttered, "Yes, Reb—um, Mrs. Nichols." I winced at my blunder. "Um, it's V."

"Excuse me?"

"Please, just call me V."

"Certainly, V," Mrs. Nichols said with a smile and continued taking roll. She was my mom's best friend and had been ever since they both began teaching here, seventeen years ago. I've known her all my life. Mom wasn't sure Rebecca (as I knew her) should be my teacher because she worried about favoritism.

When deciding which freshman English teacher's class I should be in, Mom wavered between her friend and a newer co-worker she didn't know. She ended up choosing Rebecca Nichols. She said Mrs. Nichols was strict and organized and promised not to show favoritism. Mom knew she could count on her because she was a true professional. I just needed to remember to call her Mrs. Nichols while in her class.

Mrs. Nichols went over the class syllabus, her rules and expectations for the semester, and handed out copies of *Lord of the Flies*. I worried about Emma. Twenty minutes into class and she still wasn't here.

I'd been freaking blowing up her phone for over an hour, and still nothing. *Something's wrong!* An unexplained fear squeezed my stomach as panic rose up the back of my throat like bile.

Emma and I have been friends since the first day of first grade. Literally. She walked up to me on the playground at lunchtime on the first day of school and said, "Hi, my name is Emma. Wanna be friends?" She handed me a Nutter Butter Peanut Butter Sandwich cookie and that was all it took. We've been best friends ever since. Inseparable.

We joke that we're the missing twin the other one never had. Our birthdays are even on the same day: June 24, 2001.

We do everything together, including family vacations with each other's families. I know her better than I know myself. And Emma Maria Moreno García would not miss the first day of high school unless something terrible happened.

I squeezed my eyes shut. *What if she got in an accident on the way to school? What if she's in a hospital dying right now and I'm not there for her? I need answers, not more questions! Why do I feel like this is about to be the longest day of my life?*

THE MORNING torturously ticked by like a turtle stuck in molasses. I sat through each class alternating between looking at my phone for text messages from Emma and staring at the wall clock waiting for the bell to ring. I didn't talk to anyone all morning, and I sat in the third or fourth row in every class. Not in the front row with the suck-ups, and not in the back row with the slackers, but right in the middle. I just wanted to get through the day and stay under the radar.

Each teacher droned on about classroom policies, grading procedures, and what wonderful things we had to look forward to this year. And of course, every teacher said the same thing, as if they were all reading from the same script: "I know you have other classes, but *this* class is the most important one not to miss. Your attendance is mandatory." Yeah, yeah. Whatever.

Finally, at two minutes left of fourth period, the bell was about to ring for lunch, and I had a plan.

3

FIRST DAY TURNED WORST DAY

Lunchtime—finally. With my only friend missing and no one else to hang out with, I decided to ditch. I'd miss AP World History and PE, but nothing happens the first day anyway. And I had to find Emma.

My family lived a mile from the high school, in the Old Town District of Orange, California. Living in Old Town meant we lived in an old house. Ours was built in 1918. The old homes in the area had been preserved by the historical society. It was supposed to be some kind of treasure of history. Therefore, we weren't allowed to demolish our home and start over. Walking around our neighborhood was like being transported back in time about seventy years—but with modern cars in the old driveways.

It had been mostly easy to leave school during lunchtime since we had an open campus. Upperclassmen (juniors and seniors) were allowed to go off campus during lunch. Freshmen weren't. But I wasn't about to let that little detail stop me. I spotted a tall senior boy and hid behind him, using him as a shield. When he showed the lunch aide his ID at the gate, I snuck out past them.

"Hey!" she shouted.

I turned around, thinking I'd been caught, but she was talking to someone else. "Pick that up and throw it away. The trash can is over there."

This was my chance and I took it. I ran to catch up with the others and blend in before she noticed me.

Unfortunately, I didn't know any upperclassmen willing to give me a ride. I'd have to walk. Luckily, Emma lived close. Her house was just one street over from mine, a few blocks away.

Not much of a runner, I half jogged and half walked. It took me less than fifteen minutes to get there. But I wasn't remotely prepared for what I saw when I rounded the corner to Emma's house.

Halfway down the street, right in front of her house, were two parked police cars. Panic and dread coursed through my body, and cold sweat oozed through my pores.

What the hell?

The fight-or-flight instinct kicked in, and my feet took off running for Emma's house before my brain could catch up.

Without hesitating, I burst through the front door of Emma's house like it was my own. When I entered the living room, I saw Emma's mom, Rosa. I blinked a couple times to try to make sense of what I saw.

Rosa was sobbing on the couch, while a uniformed police officer, looking uncomfortable, tried consoling her by patting her knee. No one else was in the room with them, but I heard Emma's grandma in the kitchen and another voice I didn't recognize.

"What's going on? Where's Emma? Why wasn't she in school today?" I blurted out all at once.

The police officer looked up at me. "And who are you?"

"I'm Emma's best friend, that's who!" I yelled. By this point, I wasn't in control of my emotions. I'd already had a bad day, and it rapidly worsened with every heartbeat that thudded in my ears. I needed answers. I needed Emma.

"Good, I'm glad you're here. We'll be needing to talk to you, Miss . . . ?"

"V. It's V, okay? Now will somebody please tell me what's going on?" I demanded, tears forming in my eyes.

"Emma's been taken," a man in a suit said. He walked across the room toward me and extended his right hand. "Detective Lomeli, homicide." I didn't shake his hand. He lowered his arm and scanned my face. "We need to ask you a few questions, V. When was the last time you saw Emma?"

"Taken? Homicide? What the—?" I stopped and forced myself to breathe. I gulped air. "We picked up our schedules at school yesterday, then hung out for a while. She texted me this morning, before school, to ask what I was wearing today. We made plans to wear our matching concert shirts and . . . um . . . that's all. That's the last time I heard from her. She hasn't answered her phone since. Today was the first day of school and . . ." I couldn't continue.

The reality of his words sank in. *Taken. Homicide. Taken. Homicide.*

I couldn't make my mind accept it. A thousand questions swirled in my head, yet I couldn't make my mouth move. I couldn't speak. I was in the middle of a nightmare. But I was wide awake.

"V, honey, come sit down." It was Rosa, Emma's mom. She patted the couch next to her and gestured for me to come over. "Shame on you, Detective. The poor girl's in shock. You didn't have to tell her like that. Why'd you have to say homicide? Emma's not dead!"

I sat down next to Rosa, and she hugged me tight. She continued to hold me and wouldn't let go while she soothed, "Emma's not dead. She's not dead. It's okay. We're going to find her. She's alive."

I broke away. "What happened? How do you know she's been taken? Maybe she got hit by a car and she's in the hospital, or maybe—"

"No. There was a witness." Rosa's voice shook. "A woman saw a young man shove Emma in his car. She's the one who called the police. They found Emma's phone, smashed, in the middle of the street."

"What? Where? When? Who would do this? I don't understand!"

"We're hoping you can help us with that." It was the detective again.

"Me? How would I know?"

"Was she communicating with any strangers online? Did she talk about meeting someone? Did she go to bars or—?"

"No! Nothing like that. She's not stupid. All of her followers are people that she actually knows. Instagram is all she has because she thinks social media is a waste of time. She never talks to strangers and wouldn't even dream of going into a bar. She's only fourteen."

"I had to ask. Just a formality. And you'd be surprised what some kids do at that age."

"What's that supposed to mean?"

"Just that. Are you sure you knew Emma as well as you think?"

"Stop talking about her in the past! Yes, I *know* everything about her. And she would never do those things."

"Okay, my bad. I'm on your side here—you'd do well to remember that, young lady." Lomeli took a seat in the chair next to the couch and looked at me. He continued, "Help me get to know Emma, too. The more information we have, the more leads we can follow to find her, got it?"

"Yeah, I get it. I'll tell you anything you want to know. But first, tell me what you think happened."

Detective Lomeli cleared his throat and eyed me for a minute, probably deciding how much to tell me. Then he leaned forward, elbows on his knees, and began, "Miss Moreno left this house at seven o'clock this morning. She told her mom she wanted to walk because it would help her burn off nervous energy, and she said she wanted to get there early.

"At 7:19, a woman on Cedar Avenue called the police and reported a kidnapping. She said she saw a man jump out of his parked vehicle and grab Miss Moreno. The two struggled and something fell to the ground. The suspect stomped on it, then shoved Miss Moreno into the back seat of his vehicle. He got in and sped away before the witness could make out the license plate number."

"Who's this witness? How far away was she? What kind of car? What did the guy look like?"

"V, how about you leave that part to us, deal? The sketch artist is with the witness now. As soon as we have a description, we'll release it to the media and put out an APB. We need you to tell us as much as you can about your friend."

"Like what?"

"Hobbies, interests, friends, after-school activities . . . anything you think might be useful. By the way, why aren't you in school right now?"

"I left at lunch because my best friend is missing. Are you going to arrest me for truancy?"

"Not this time," Lomeli said and winked. "But, V?"

"What?"

"You need to go to school tomorrow, okay?"

"Why?"

"Because you're a kid, and that's what kids are supposed to do. Stay in school, get educated, and take your mind off this case. Let us do our jobs and we'll find your friend."

4

VERONICA MARS

Detective Lomeli's words echoed in my mind. *"Stay in school, get educated, and take your mind off this case. Let us do our jobs and we'll find your friend."*

Yeah, right. My best friend has just been kidnapped and I'm supposed to go to school like everything's normal? I'm supposed to not think about it? Does this guy even have a clue?

I'm not only going to think about this case, I'm going to solve this case. I'm going to find Emma. After all, I don't just go by V because I don't like the name Violet.

My parents named me Violet Hemingway Jiménez. Violet is my grandmother's middle name (my mom's mom), Hemingway is my mom's favorite author (because she's a nerdy English teacher; my little brother's name is Scott Fitzgerald Jiménez), and Jiménez because my dad, Carlos Jiménez, is from Costa Rica.

My parents' students call them Mr. and Mrs. J. It started sixteen years ago when a student in one of my dad's classes was a big fan of LL Cool J, the rapper. He called my dad Mr. J in class one day by saying, "You're so cool, Mr. J . . . just like LL Cool J." The kids loved it, and the name stuck. The rest, as they say, is history. Get what I did there? *History.* Because my dad's a history teacher! Ha ha. Okay, I admit it. I'm a nerd, too.

Anyway, I liked the idea of a nickname or shortened name but didn't want to be called Vi. Emma came up with V last year when we became *Veronica Mars* fans, also known as "marshmallows." I loved it and have been trying to get everyone to call me V since.

WHO IS VERONICA MARS? Only the greatest teen detective ever! Okay, so she's not real. She's a fictional character from the *Veronica Mars* TV series that ran for three seasons. It first aired in 2004.

Veronica is a new-and-improved version of Nancy Drew. She's like Philip Marlowe, Columbo, Sherlock Holmes, *and* Nancy Drew all rolled into one. She may not be a superhero, but she is definitely one tough badass you don't want to mess with.

Anyway, I was only three years old when the show first aired. But my mom was a fan and found the whole series on DVD at a garage sale a couple years ago. Mom loved sharing memorabilia and classic movies and "cultural icons" she thought I should know about from her era. She instilled a love for nostalgia in me, so when she introduced me to another of her favorite things, I was all for it. We started binge watching the *Veronica Mars* series together before the movie came out last year.

It was really cool because the *Veronica Mars* movie was funded by fans of the series from a Kickstarter campaign. I even donated! It was a great feeling to know I helped make the movie possible, even if I did only donate twenty dollars. I just loved how the fans rallied together and raised enough money to get the movie made.

Mom, Emma, and I stayed up late many nights watching the episodes. We even talked about writing fanfiction. We kicked around some wild ideas. We were going to call ours *Victoria Jupiter*. It was so much fun.

And then for spring break last year, Mom surprised Emma and me with a trip to Chicago. We got to be extras on the set of *The Boss* and meet Kristen Bell! Can you believe it?

It was the highlight of my life! I got to meet the actress who plays "Anna," from *Frozen,* and Veronica Mars! She is crazy talented!

How did I get so lucky? I told you my mom's cool. She has a friend who hires kids for movies all the time. She works at a big extras casting agency in Burbank called Kids Management. She heard they needed kids for a film they were shooting in Chicago, and that Kristen Bell was going to be in it.

It was easy to sell it to Mom. First, my mom has always wanted to visit Chicago because she has a cousin who lives there. Second, they were filming the kid scenes during our spring break so we wouldn't miss any school, and third, I'm a huge fan of Kristen Bell.

Emma and I were issued entertainment work permits and hired to play "Dandelions," the film's version of Girl Scouts. Not only did we get to meet and take selfies with Kristen (who is super nice and awesome!) we got to have a couple of fun days of filming and hanging out on a movie set—and we made $162 a day! We would have done it for free.

And now, there's a real case. My one and only friend in the entire world has been kidnapped. And I'm going to be the one who finds her. This is my chance.

I'm going to be a teenage private eye—just like Veronica Mars.

5

THE C WORD

Two days later—the third day of school.

I decided to take Detective Lomeli's advice after all and went back to school yesterday. I mean, how could I solve Emma's case if I stayed home?

Mom wouldn't let me watch the news or read any newspapers. I guess she was trying to protect me, but there was no protecting me from the news of Emma's kidnapping—it was all over the school.

Dr. Sykes, the school psychologist, called me into her office twice. The first time was to make sure I wasn't traumatized, and she asked me if I wanted to talk about it. The second time was to send me home because she didn't believe me when I told her I wasn't traumatized but didn't want to talk about it.

"Violet, I think you need to accept that Emma might be gone," Dr. Sykes said.

"Gone? Of course she's 'gone,' as in, she's not here. But she's not gone like you're saying. Geez, she's only been missing twenty-eight hours and you're ready to write her off? You think she's dead? What kind of counselor are you? She's alive. I know she is. And I'm going to find her."

"Violet, you mean the police are going to find her. Right?"

"Right. Sure, whatever you say. And don't call me Violet. It's V." I got up and stormed out of her office.

I don't need to be analyzed right now. I've got better things to do.

That was yesterday. Today wasn't much better. Everyone at school treats me like I'm contagious. Like, if they talk to me they'll go missing, too. I hear them whispering when I walk by.

Whatever. I just want this day to be over so I can interview Mrs. Lee. I finally found out the name of the only witness—thanks to good ol' Google. *Did my mom really think she could keep me in a bubble?*

At lunch, I'd logged on to a library computer and watched a video from KTLA, one of the local news stations. The reporter visited the scene of the crime. He said he couldn't reveal the identity of the witness, but the idiot stood in front of her house during his on-camera standup.

Behind him, I could see a mailbox with a name on it, but I couldn't read it. No problem Google Earth's street view couldn't solve. I was able to read "LEE" on the mailbox, then cross-referenced it with the white pages, and found a Ji-yeon Lee at 913 Cedar Avenue.

Sweet! Find the witness. Check! This detective stuff is a piece of cake. I smiled and congratulated myself on solving the first clue.

With the help of that video and an article I found from *The Orange County Register* online, I now knew as much as them. The suspect was a white male, 18-28, with short, dirty blond hair and a thick build, possibly five-foot-ten. He was last seen wearing a red baseball cap, black T-shirt, and sagging jeans. The suspect drove away in an older model gray Ford SUV.

They showed a picture of Emma. I recognized it instantly

from a picture she had posted on Instagram last week at the beach. I knew it well. After all, I was the one who snapped the photo.

Emma has thick, lustrous, long black hair; big, dark brown eyes; dazzling dimples; full lips; and a smooth, red-brown skin tone. She's gorgeous, and I've always been secretly jealous of her flawless skin and complexion.

Me? My skin is half a shade darker than white, with a smattering of tiny freckles across my nose.

The bell rang for fifth period, and I jumped. I'd forgotten where I was for a minute. I'd been lost in thought, remembering that day at the beach.

We always had so much fun together.

I have to find her. I just have to. And she has to be okay!

I refused to let myself think anything else.

I WENT to Mom's classroom after school and was greeted by her substitute teacher.

"May I help you?" She looked up from the note she was writing and waited.

"Do you know where Mrs. J is? She's my mom, and I need a ride home from school."

"Oh, no, sorry dear. They didn't tell me when I took the call. She left at lunch, I only subbed for her last two classes."

"Okay, thanks." I left Mom's classroom and walked to Dad's. I remembered they took separate cars today and I rode in with Mom.

His door was locked.

"Crap. They forgot me." I sighed, cinched up my backpack

and started the mile walk home. It was 3:05 p.m. on September 3rd and hellishly hot outside. The weather app on my phone registered 106 degrees.

Figures. What else could go wrong?

By the time I got home, both my parents' cars were in the driveway. *They really did forget me.* Now I was even more upset because my feelings were hurt, too.

I opened the front door and paused in the doorway as I heard the sound of my mom crying. That was not a sound I was used to hearing. My mom was sunny, optimistic, and tough as nails. She never cried.

I sighed. *Maybe she heard news about Emma. Oh no! This can't be good.*

I ran into the living room. "Mom? What's wrong? Is it Emma? Did they find her? Is she d-dead?"

"No, honey. It's not about Emma." Mom dried her eyes and put on her serious face. I'd seen that face before. Good news never followed after she put on that face. "Sit down, V. We need to talk to you."

I looked at Dad. He sat on the couch next to Mom. His expression was blank, unreadable.

"No, that's okay, I think I'll stand. What is it, Mom? Tell me."

Silence.

"Just tell me, please. Whatever it is, I can take it. Spill it already."

"Remember that doctor appointment I had last week?" she finally managed.

"No," I said slowly as I blinked at her. *Where is she going with this?*

"Oh. Well, I got some tests done . . . and the results came back today."

"And?" My patience grew thin. "Mom, why are you being so dramatic? Oh my gosh, it's not like you have cancer."

"Actually, sweetie, it's funny you should say that . . ."

Our eyes locked.

"I'm afraid I received some bad news today," she whispered. "It turns out I do have canc—"

"WHAT? Mom, I was kidding. There's no way you can have cancer!"

"Oh? Why is that?"

"Because, only old people get cancer," I argued.

"Ah, how I wish that were true." She took a deep breath. "V, please sit down. It strains my neck to look up at you like this."

I sat down next to her, my brain numbing at what I was hearing.

"You know I'm a straight shooter, so here goes." She gave my hand a light squeeze. "I have stage four breast cancer. They want me to start chemotherapy right away, followed by radiation, followed by surgery. Then I'll do a round of hormone therapy and will participate in clinical trials."

"NO!" I screamed. "How can this be happening?" I burst into tears. "Mom, how are you so calm? How long have you known?"

"I found out at 12:30 today, so about three hours now."

"What does stage four mean? Are you going to die?"

"Well . . . everybody dies eventually, sweetheart."

I glared at her.

"The truth is, I don't know. Stage four is the worst stage. It's the most advanced cancer a person can have. They consider it terminal, but some people can live many, many years with a prognosis of terminal."

"Oh my God, noooo! Mommy!"

I threw my arms around her. We held each other and

sobbed together. Dad joined us and the three of us just held on. All I could think about in that moment was how much I loved my parents, how much I loved my mom. I couldn't lose her. No, this was some cruel joke. The doctor had it wrong. I just couldn't lose her.

I disentangled myself from my parents and sat back. I met my mom's eyes and whispered, "How long?"

"They don't know. Every case is different. If my body responds well to the chemo and I follow all the treatments, I could have many years left."

"How many is many?"

"They didn't want to put a number on it, but who knows? Maybe twenty."

"You'll die from cancer in twenty years?"

"I don't know, honey. Nobody knows."

"And if you don't do any of the treatments? If you don't get the surgery?"

"That's not an option. Of course I'm going to do all the treatments. I'm going to fight—"

"That's not what I meant. I mean, if you couldn't fight. Or if you didn't believe in western medicine and just sort of ignored it, how long would you have?"

"The doctor said that if I do absolutely nothing I'll be dead in a year."

I gasped.

"But that's not going to happen, so don't even think you're getting rid of me that easily, missy. I'm throwing everything I have into this fight, and I'm going to buy some more damn time."

THREE HOURS LATER, Mom's friend (also my English teacher) Rebecca Nichols brought Scotty home. She'd kept him with her two kids all afternoon to give us time to prepare. She also brought a pizza over for our family.

We'd discussed how much to tell Scotty, and Mom decided to tell him right away. She didn't want him hearing it from someone else, and she knew it would be public knowledge soon enough. Plus, she believed in transparency and always told us the truth. Surprisingly, he took it well. Maybe he was just too young to process it.

"So you have the C word?" Scotty asked.

"Honey, it's okay to say cancer. It's not a dirty word," Mom encouraged.

"But Alex calls it the C word." Alex was Scotty's best friend, and Scotty thought that kid walked on water.

"Why does Alex call it the C word?" Mom asked.

"Because that's what he heard his grandma call it."

"Well, I think that's because cancer is a scary word for some people and they're afraid to say it, so they call it the C word."

"Why is it scary?"

"It's not, sweetie. Cancer is just a word. If you're afraid to say it, you give the word too much power."

"I'm not afraid to say it! Cancer! Cancer, cancer, cancer!" Scotty shouted.

"That's it, good for you, li'l man!" Dad high-fived him, picked him up, and gave him a big hug. We all laughed, thankful for the distraction.

Mom continued, "The doctor told me we need to keep life as normal as possible. That means we go to school and work and stick to our routines the best we can. According to the cancer pamphlets they gave me, the structure is supposed to help."

Normal? What a joke. What the hell about my life is normal? My best friend has been kidnapped, and my mom has CANCER. I've had three lousy days of high school so far and made zero new friends. The two other friends I had in eighth grade go to the other high school in our district, and I haven't talked to them all summer. Emma and I are the only two from our small circle of friends who go to Sierra—except she's not here to go to Sierra with me.

I literally have no one to talk to about this. Plus, Mom asked me not to tell anyone yet because she doesn't know when she's going to tell Dr. Fitz. She knows she's going to need time off for treatments, and she doesn't want to lose her job.

Life, as I know it, SUCKS.

6

HAPPY BIRTHDAY, MOM

My alarm blared at six o'clock the next morning to the tune of "Misery," by Maroon 5. I changed it from the perky "Cheerleader," by OMI, because I needed something that matched my mood better. It didn't quite work, but it was closer than what I usually listened to. It's still an upbeat tune but with dark lyrics.

That's me in a nutshell. I'm upbeat and well adjusted on the outside but plotting the demise of whoever kidnapped Emma—and whoever gave my mom cancer—on the inside. Someone's responsible, and they're going to pay.

By the way, today is Friday, September 4, 2015, and the fourth day of school.

It's also my mom's 39th birthday. *Happy birthday, Hannah Jiménez. Have some cancer for your special day. Surprise!*

That's right, she found out she had cancer the *day before* her birthday. What kind of reverse poetic justice is that?

Look, I'm not saying my mom is perfect. Of course she's not—no one is. But she's a good person, and she doesn't deserve this. She's kind and funny, feisty and quirky, wicked smart, and a friend to all who know her. She has taught and inspired thousands of students at SHS. And she's the best mom I could have ever hoped for.

Mom grew up here, born and raised. Ironically, she went to our rival school—Orange High School. Then she went to San Diego State University on a tennis scholarship. She traveled all over playing tennis in college, and many people thought she'd go pro.

But an injury at a match her sophomore year stopped that dream. I'm a little fuzzy on the details; it's been years since I heard that story. Anyway, her other loves were reading and literature—so she decided to become an English teacher. She graduated, came back home, and got a teaching job right away at Sierra. She's been there ever since.

At new teacher orientation, Mom said she was just sitting there minding her own business when the hottest guy in the world walked through the door. She didn't know who he was and had never met him before, but she knew she was going to marry him. That man was my dad. Of course, she tells the story much better. She adds details and gross stuff I'm not comfortable talking about. I mean, he's my *dad!* Geez.

Anyway, she said the whole first year they dated they had to keep it a secret because teachers weren't allowed to date each other. Some district policy about employee fraternization. They had to go out to dinner at faraway restaurants and couldn't be seen shopping for groceries together. When you work and live in the same town, you run into your students everywhere.

One night, she and Dad were at a restaurant in Santa Monica, a good fifty miles away, when a student spotted them kissing. That's all it took. The news was all over the school the next day.

"Miss Kelly and Mr. J were caught making out at Tallula's"

may as well have been the headline in the school newspaper that day. They were both first-year teachers and already popular. The kids loved them because they were young and cool. Mom was 22, and Dad was 23.

Dad proposed that night. By the time administration got wind of it, they were officially engaged and weren't in violation of their contracts anymore. They found the loophole. Co-workers weren't allowed to date, but the contracts didn't say anything about being engaged or married.

They got married during Christmas break the next school year, December 28, 1999. I was born a year and a half later.

Mom said she had loved all the sneaking around they'd had to do. It was a grand adventure and exciting to keep coming up with new ideas for secret outings.

They still surprise each other with adventures and impromptu weekend getaways. Mom says it's what keeps the fires burning and the romance alive. I see the way Dad still looks at her. I never thought much about it before, but my parents are still in love.

And since it's Mom's birthday, Labor Day weekend, and she was just given the worst news of her life yesterday, Dad surprised her with one of his spontaneous trips. As soon as the bell rang at the end of the day, he waltzed into her classroom and whisked her away.

THEY DECIDED I was still too young to be left alone, especially for a three-day weekend, so they got Grandma Kelly to stay with me. This was new. All the other times when they went out of town, Scotty stayed with his friend Alex while I stayed with Emma.

Well, Scotty still got to stay with Alex. But, yay me, I got Grandma. Don't get me wrong, my mom's mom is great, and I love her—but she treats me like a kid. I have to find a way to lose the leash so I can find Emma this weekend. I'm going to need to be very creative.

During dinner, I came up with a plan. "Grandma?" I said in the sweetest voice I could muster.

"Yes, dear?" she said, equally sweet.

"I have a huge history project to do this weekend and need to go to the library to do some research," I lied. "I don't want to bother you, so I'll just ride my bike over there, okay?"

"It's no bother, dear. I can give you a ride to the library. But can't you do your research on your computer? On that Internet, like the kids do these days?"

"Actually, believe it or not, encyclopedias are still best for some things. Besides, the downtown library has a great study atmosphere and really helps me focus."

Hey, I think I'm getting good at this lying thing. The truth was, I'd never been to the downtown library. But I knew Grandma would let me go there over just about anywhere else because education and good grades were expected in my family. Since *both* my parents were teachers, the pressure was on. Thankfully, learning came naturally to me and I had a near perfect GPA.

"Did you know my father owned a full set of encyclopedias when I was your age? They were his pride and joy. Even though I could read them whenever I wanted, I enjoyed going to the library myself. You're right. There's just something about that environment . . . with all those books. How about if I drive you over after we clear the table and do the dishes?"

"Well, I was hoping to ride my bike, if you don't mind. And

I'd like to go now so I can be back before dark. I was looking forward to the fresh air and exercise."

"All right, go on then. I get it. You know, your ol' grandma was young once, too." She smiled and winked at me, then kissed my forehead. "But take a sweater. It might get chilly."

"Grandma, it's still eighty-nine degrees outside. It won't get *chilly* until November."

"Oh, all right, miss smarty-pants. Be off with you then." She laughed.

7

WITNESS

I rode my bike four blocks to Cedar Avenue—the scene of the crime. It was the first time I'd been on that street since Emma's kidnapping.

I slowed down and decided to get off my bike and walk. I scanned the street for clues. I don't know what I was looking for, exactly, but if Emma lost a bracelet or an earring, or even a hair band, I was determined to find it.

No such luck.

It was time to talk to Mrs. Lee.

I rang the doorbell at 913 Cedar Avenue, an old white house with a creaky front porch.

An elderly woman with short salt-and-pepper hair answered the door.

"Hello, ma'am, are you Mrs. Lee?" I asked.

"Yes. May I help you?"

"Yes, ma'am. I'm a reporter for *The Sun Gazette* and would like to ask you a few questions about the kidnapping you witnessed a few days ago."

"Oh? Too young to be newspaper reporter, aren't you?" she

squinted at me through her glasses. I detected a strong accent and wasn't sure how much English she understood. For some reason, I spoke louder, as if I thought somehow that would help.

"Oh, thank you. I get that all the time. I'm actually twenty—"

"Save it, dearie. I not born yesterday. Just because you see old Korean woman, you think I stupid, yes?"

"No, of course not. I just—"

"I saw you ride up and hide bike behind that bush." She pointed at the bush on her next-door neighbor's property. "Reporter no ride bike. Right? Where is your press badge, then, huh? You think you fool me? You look twelve-year-old. Now, what you want?"

"I . . . uh . . . well—"

"I no have all night. Out with it. And tell the truth. I know if you lie to me. Who are you?"

Darn it! It always worked for Veronica Mars.

I looked down at my dirty Converse sneakers and sighed. Who was I kidding? I knew I didn't look like an adult. Not even close. I was five feet tall and scrawny. My scale showed I'd hit triple digits just last week. Finally, an even hundred pounds.

Mrs. Lee was right, with a few freckles scattered across my nose and cheeks, I definitely looked like a twelve-year-old. Probably even younger, considering I had no breasts or hips yet. In fact, I was still waiting for my period to start. How did I think I was going to pull this off?

When all else fails, try the truth? Here goes nothing.

"My name is Violet Jiménez. The girl you saw being shoved into that SUV three days ago is my best friend. The police haven't found her yet, and they're not telling me anything. I have to find her. Please, you have to help me."

"How you find me? I ask police not say my name."

"I saw a news clip on the Internet. The reporter was standing in front of your mailbox, in front of your house. I went to street view on Google and zoomed in on the mailbox. It said 'LEE' on it. I looked in the white pages of the phonebook for a Lee on Cedar Avenue. You were the only one. Your address was listed."

"Hmm, smart girl. Okay, come in. I help you."

"Thank you! Thank you so much. Anything you could tell me would be very helpful. I just need to make sense out of all this. Who would want to take Emma?"

"I don't know. But you tell truth, so now I tell you what I tell police. Come. Sit. You want tea?"

"No thank you." I sat down on the blue floral sofa and looked around.

Mrs. Lee eyed me. "Water?"

"I'm sorry?"

"Water. You want water?"

"I'm fine, thank you. Really. I just want to know what you saw that morning."

"Okay. I tell you. Sorry, it is not much." She sat in the matching armchair across from where I sat on the sofa. She took a deep breath, cleared her throat, and then waited.

Is she thinking?

The silence grew awkward. Finally, Mrs. Lee spoke. "You sure you not want tea? No trouble."

Losing patience, I gritted my teeth. "Yes, I'm sure. I'm sorry to rush you, Mrs. Lee, but it is going to be dark soon, and I promised my grandmother I'd be home before dark. Can you please just tell me what you saw?"

"Oh, you have grandmother stay with you? That nice. I have grandkids, too. They all grow up now."

I squirmed and tried to smile, but it was getting to be too much. *Is this lady ever going to tell me anything?*

"Okay, I tell you now. But don't get hope up, kid. I not see much. It was early. I not wear my glasses yet. I not see license plate on car. Everything fuzzy."

"But you saw the guy, right? The guy who took Emma?"

"Yes. I see the guy. I put kettle on stove. I hear a scream. I look out my window but not see anyone. I open front door and go out on porch. I see guy push girl in car. Two houses down street, that way." She pointed to the right. "I see only back of car. Young guy walk around to front of car, get in driver side, peel out fast."

"Car? I thought it was an SUV?"

"What? Oh yes, yes. American car. SUV. Big car. Big gray car. SUV."

"How do you know he's young?"

"He wear baseball cap low, over face. His pants sag down around his backside like gang kids wear."

"You think he's a gang member?"

"I don't know. But his pants sag down low like gang kids."

"What color was the baseball cap?"

"Oh, did I not mention? Red. And he wear black T-shirt."

"Did you see his shoes?"

"No. All happen too fast. I try to look at license plate when he drive away with girl. She scream. She scream a lot, so I call police."

My breath caught in my throat. I imagined Emma screaming. I imagined her scared and fighting for her life.

Get a grip. I have to see what else she knows.

"Why did the guy walk around the SUV? Did he put her in the passenger side?"

"Yes. They on my side of street, parked facing that a way."

She gestured to her right. "Passenger side on curb. He must be sitting in passenger seat waiting for girl walk by. When she come, he jump out and grab her. He push her in back seat. He walk around front to driver side and drive away."

"Is there anything else you remember? Anything else you can think of to tell me?"

"Girl struggle and drop something. I think her phone. Guy stomp on it and kick it away. Police find phone in middle of street."

"What about his voice? Was it deep? Did he have an accent?"

"I not hear him. I think he must whisper to her. He speak very quiet."

"What about his skin color?"

"White."

"Hair?"

"Short and yellow."

"You mean blond?"

"Yes. Blond."

"Thank you, Mrs. Lee." I stood up to leave. "Thank you so much for talking to me and telling me what you saw. Thank you for calling the police."

"I sorry about your friend. I wish I see license plate to help catch bad guy."

"I know you do. It's okay. It's not your fault. We'll catch him. Don't worry."

"We?"

"I mean the police, of course."

"I give you advice. I nice. You talk to me, is okay. But no talk to bad guys. Let police do. No pretend reporter. No more stranger. You must be careful. Understand?"

"I . . . I think so."

"Is dangerous for you." She reached for my hand and patted it. "Not a game. No Nancy Drew. Bad guy real. Stay away. I not want see you in trouble."

"I understand, Mrs. Lee. Don't worry. I'll be very careful, I promise. Thank you again for your time. I better get back before my grandma gets worried. Good night."

THE PORCH LIGHT was on when I rode up and put my bike in the garage. It was 7:31 p.m. and the sun had just disappeared over the horizon.

"Violet?" Grandma sounded worried. "You said you'd be home before dark."

"It's not dark yet. It's dusk," I joked. "And call me V, please."

"It's dark enough, *Violet*. I suppose you think you're too good for the family name now? Violet is my middle name, you know. And Violet was my mother's name. *Your* mother named you Violet, so that is how I shall address you—by your given name."

I rolled my eyes but knew better than to argue with her.

"And I do not think you should be out this late, given the circumstances. You were out there all alone on a bicycle, riding around at night. What would your parents think? What if something had happened to you?"

I couldn't help myself. I snapped. "Oh, you mean I could get kidnapped, LIKE EMMA DID? Who, by the way, was taken IN BROAD DAYLIGHT! I don't really think the time of day is relevant. Do *you*, Grandma?"

"Watch your tone, missy. I know this is a difficult time for you, Violet. You miss your friend very much, and you have every right to be upset, but that doesn't give you the right to disrespect me or be sassy. Is that clear?"

"Yes, Grandma. I'm sorry."

"All right then. Now how about we put on a fun, light-hearted movie, and eat the chocolate chip cookies I just made. Hmm?" she said with a twinkle in her eye.

I fell into her arms and let her hold me while I cried. Chocolate chip cookies wouldn't solve my problems, and they definitely wouldn't find Emma, but they sounded like a good ending to a very long, very emotional day.

8

SLOW DAY IN GEOMETRY

Grandma kept a close watch on me the rest of the weekend. And when I asked to ride my bike, she reminded me of my very own words: "Kids get taken during daylight hours, too." She remained steadfast. "If you're going to get yourself kidnapped, it won't be on my watch." Once Grandma made her mind up, there was no changing it.

I managed to accept the terms of my three-day house arrest and used the time to be productive. I thoroughly cleaned my room, organized my closet, went through my clothes, and filled a couple trash bags with clothes that didn't fit me anymore to take to the local women's shelter. They always needed kids' clothes.

I also got caught up on all my homework, and even wrote a research paper for AP World History that wasn't due for another week. I'd never had so much free time on my hands before. Yet, even these tasks weren't enough to distract me from my thoughts.

I miss Emma so much!

"V! V! WHERE ARE YOU?" Scotty called as he ran through the house. He found me in my bedroom. Apparently, Mom and Dad picked him up on their way home from their little getaway.

"V! Wait till you see Mommy!" Scotty shouted from my doorway. "You're gonna flip. Come on!" He grabbed my hand and led me downstairs. I was afraid to ask what he meant.

I let Scotty lead me to the kitchen, where we saw Grandma talking to Dad and a lady with short red hair. I couldn't get a good look at her, but from the back, she looked like Mom. She turned to face me. It was Mom!

My hands shot to my face. I tried to disguise my shock. Mom's beautiful long hair had always been her pride and joy. People complimented her on it and often told her it looked like a lion's mane—her crowning glory. I stared at her new bobbed-at-the-chin haircut as my mouth gaped open.

Scotty laughed and pointed at me. "I told you! Ha ha. You should see the look on your face right now!"

"Well hello, daughter," Mom greeted me.

I just stood there.

"Cat got your tongue?" she asked, winking. "What's the matter? Don't you like it? I call it my preemptive cut. You know, cut it short before it all falls out."

"Yeah, and Mommy said she's gonna let me help her cut all her hair off when it starts to fall out from the chemo. She's gonna be bald!" Scotty exclaimed.

"I love it," I managed. "I think it looks great." I walked over and hugged her tight.

After a moment, she gently pushed me away and said, "I'm starving. What's for dinner?"

"I've got a tuna casserole in the oven. It's almost done," Grandma said. "And I like your hair, too, Hannah. It suits you."

We had a nice family dinner together, talking and laughing and getting caught up on each other's weekends. But I watched Mom as she ate. I tried to picture her bald and shuddered at the thought.

After dinner, I cleared the table and started the dishes while Grandma chatted in the living room with my parents. They spoke in soft tones, and I couldn't hear their conversation.

Scotty stayed at the kitchen table. He played on his iPad, oblivious to the world.

Dishes done, I dried my hands and walked into the living room. Grandma sat on the couch, holding Mom close.

I heard Grandma say, "Hannah, darling, you know I would give anything to trade places with you, to make this all go away for you and your family, to make everything better."

"I know, Mom. I know," Mom whispered. She looked up and saw me standing there. They quickly broke away.

Grandma stood up, all business, and announced, "Well, look at the time. I'd better head on home now. Violet, I loved spending time with you this weekend. Come give Grandma a kiss."

"It was good to hang with you, too, Grandma." I hugged her and she held me a little too tight. She kissed me on the cheek and stepped back, her eyes glistening with tears.

Grandma gave Mom and Dad a quick smile, then walked into the kitchen to say bye to Scotty. I was on my way up to my room when I heard the front door close, signaling that Grandma was on her way back to her own house ten miles away in Yorba Linda.

It was good to have my family back, but by Tuesday morning, I was ready to go to school again. I needed the distraction.

Tuesday morning also meant that it had been a full week since Emma had been taken. Even though her mom had gone on TV to plead for information, no one had called in.

The only witness was Mrs. Lee. The kidnappers made no demands. There was no ransom request. No contact. As far as I knew, there were no leads. The police were no closer to finding Emma than I was.

I WALKED through the poster-lined hallways on my way to first period, thoughts of Emma consuming me. Honors English. It was the one class Emma and I were supposed to have together.

The different variations of red, white, and black paint on butcher paper announced Club Week.

They were full of school spirit and Wylie the Warrior pride. *Not to be confused with Wile E. Coyote.* I laughed to myself, still loving the old, classic Warner Bros. cartoons.

Each poster touted their club superior over all the other clubs.

If Emma were here, which club would she join?

Emma had more school spirit than I did. She would've talked me into joining a club or two.

Probably something awful like Spirit Club. Ew. I shuddered for show, even though no one around me paid the slightest attention.

I didn't have any friends, so I had to amuse myself somehow. It was either that or wallow in a pit of despair. I might not be 'peppy,' but at least I tried to maintain a mostly positive outlook on life—even when my best friend was who knows where right now.

I had AP Bio after English, then French 1, then Geometry. Madame Côté raved on and on about French Club. She told us how juniors got to go to Paris in the exchange student program.

I was sort of interested. I mean, I've wanted to visit France ever since I saw *Hugo* a few years ago. I especially wanted to climb to the top of the Eiffel Tower. But to qualify for the trip, I'd have to sign up for three years of French classes.

I don't want to commit to taking three years of French right now. I don't even like French 1 yet.

Besides, a trip to Paris was something I'd want to take with Emma. I couldn't imagine going overseas, or anywhere really, without her.

By the time I got to Geometry, I was ready for this day to end. It wasn't even lunchtime yet. *Sigh.*

I walked into Geometry to find a sub waiting for us. After the tardy bell rang, she took roll and marked anyone absent who wasn't sitting in his or her assigned seat. She wrote her name on the board, "Miss Tasker," gave a little speech about no talking, follow the classroom rules, blah blah blah, handed out the assignment, and told us to work independently. Then she went over to Mr. Goodenough's desk and logged on to his computer.

Yes, you read that right; my math teacher's name is Mr. Goodenough. He made fun of it himself the first day of school. He told us a sad story about how he was picked on as a kid because of his name. Other kids said he was never "good enough" for anything. The whole class felt sorry for him, so no one snickered or teased him about his name. He was actually pretty cool.

Most of us finished the assignment early and were already bored. We watched the clock, waiting impatiently for the lunch bell to ring. Jacob, stocky with a crew cut and baseball cap, waved his arms wildly. Shelly, sitting next to him, couldn't stop giggling. "Stop it," she said in between giggles.

"Why you actin' so weird? Stop talkin' freaky shit," Jacob said.

"I'm not. Knock it off," Shelly protested.

"Great. Now she's lookin' at me." Jacob motioned toward Miss Tasker. "You snitch. Take that." He snapped his lanyard in the air an inch from Shelly's face. "I'm calling security."

Shelly blushed and laughed, then said, "Stop it," repeatedly amidst her giggle fits. I rolled my eyes.

Does she enjoy the attention? Is she embarrassed? Does she like him?

Just as I began to analyze the situation (What else was there to do?), Miss Tasker finally got up from the desk and walked over to Jacob. She didn't know his name, so she stood in front of him and said, "Put your lanyard away."

"I didn't touch her. She's all drama," Jacob said in mock protest.

"Just put it away," Miss Tasker repeated and sighed, hands on her hips. She gave him a final look, then turned and walked back to the teacher's desk. She disappeared once more behind the computer monitor.

Jacob shoved his lanyard in his backpack with dramatic flair. Just then, an office aide walked in with a note and gave it to Jacob. He pushed his chair back, making as much noise as possible and stated, "Hey, teach. I gotta go. Coach needs me."

Without taking her eyes off the computer screen, Miss Tasker said, "Fine. Make sure you take your backpack." Jacob made more noise, picked up his backpack, and left.

Across the room, Brylee took a multicolored headband and wrapped it around Kevin's big curly mop top. She made a little ponytail on top of his head. He even tilted his head down to make it easier for her.

He clearly likes the attention. I wonder what's up with those two.

Two boys I didn't know wrote dirty words on the extra whiteboard in the back of the room. One drew an outline of a 'penis and balls.'

Classy.

Another kid spun a quarter on his desk, over and over.

OMG, how much longer? Somebody save me, please! Will this class ever end?

Another aide walked in with a note and gave it to Miss Tasker. She read it. She cleared her throat and said, "Violet Jiménez? You're wanted in the office."

Thank you! My plea has been answered!

I grabbed my backpack and walked up to the teacher's desk so Miss Tasker could hand me the note. It said Dr. Sykes wanted to see me.

Hmm. Well, at least it gets me out of Geometry.

"HOW ARE YOU DOING TODAY, V?" Dr. Sykes asked.

"Fine. How are you doing today, Dr. Sykes?" I mimicked.

"Actually, V, I'm concerned about you." She paused and shuffled some papers on her desk. "Emma's been gone a week now, and I think we need to work on some coping strategies to help get you through this."

"Coping strategies? To help me get through what?" I narrowed my eyes and tensed my jaw.

"V, you need to prepare yourself for the fact that Emma

might not come back. The longer a kidnap victim is missing, the less likely it is that—"

"I know! Don't say it." My eyes watered, and I blinked away tears.

"There are excellent grief support groups and programs I can refer you to. I think they'd be very good for you. It helps to have an outlet for your grief, someone you can talk to. Since you won't talk to me—"

"I won't talk to you because there's nothing to talk about," I snapped. "And I'm not grieving. Emma's still out there. I know it. I can feel it. And I'm going to find her." I got up and stormed out of Dr. Sykes's office.

9

SHARMEL

I had to walk home again, but this time my parents included me in the loop. Today was Mom's first day of chemotherapy, and she'd be there a couple more hours. I decided to make dinner to surprise her.

"V, we're home," Dad called from the front door. "Will you come out here, please?"

I ran outside to greet them, "Hey, Dad, what's up?"

"We stopped by the store and got a few recommended items. Will you take them in the house while I take your mother upstairs? The chemo made her nauseous, and she doesn't feel so good."

"Okay, but I made dinner for her, her favorite—"

"Um, thanks honey. That was sweet of you, but she won't be able to eat anything tonight. I'm sure it will still taste great tomorrow." Dad walked around to the passenger side and helped Mom out. She looked pale and weak.

"Hi Mom. Where's Scotty?" I filled in the awkward silence with the only thing I could think of.

"He's spending the night at Alex's tonight. I don't want him wearing your mother out," Dad answered.

"You can't keep sending him away every time Mom has a—"

"I realize that, V. Just get the stuff, will you?"

Dad was rarely ever cross and almost never raised his voice. I watched him take Mom in the house.

This is hard on him, too. Man, this sucks!

THE NEXT DAY, while we were at school, Mom stayed home to rest. Another exciting day for me—not. When Dad and I got home, there was a car we didn't recognize in the driveway. We walked in the house and overheard Dr. Sykes talking to Mom in the living room.

"What's *she* doing here?" I grumbled.

"You don't like Molly?" Dad chuckled. "We've worked with her for ten years. She may seem gruff, but Molly's the real deal, and she genuinely cares about the kids. You'd be hard-pressed to find another human being who cares more about our students than Molly."

"It's not that I don't like her . . . it's just that she calls me to her office all the time to talk about Emma. I don't want to talk about Emma! She won't leave me alone about it."

"How dare she?" He reacted in mock indignation. "You mean she's doing her job? Shocker."

"Whatever, Dad." I rolled my eyes. "I don't have to go in there and talk to her, do I?"

"Of course you don't, and neither do I," he said. "She's here to see your mother anyway, so I'm going out to the garage for a bit, then I'll swing by Alex's and pick up Scotty." Dad winked at me and walked toward the garage.

"And I'm going to my room." I winked back. We smiled at each other and went our separate ways.

I heard something on my way upstairs that stopped me mid step. Hidden by the wall, I turned around and sat down on the stairs to listen.

"I'm worried about V. She thinks Emma is still out there, still alive," Dr. Sykes said.

"And you don't?" Mom asked.

"I'm sorry, but . . . no, I don't. Statistically, when strangers abduct children, they fall into one of three categories. The kidnappers either abduct and kill them, hold them for ransom, or take them with the intention to keep them.

"There have been no ransom demands, and Emma is not the targeted age to 'keep and raise.' I'm afraid that leaves the third category. And if that's true, the abductors are most likely to kill their victim within the first twenty-four to forty-eight hours of the abduction."

"Molly, that's terrible. But what if Emma's case is different? What if—"

Dr. Sykes cut Mom off and continued, "I also know from personal experience that hope is futile. When I was V's age, something similar happened to me. We didn't have proper grief counseling back then, like we do now. I never got to talk about it, never got the help I needed. It still haunts me, which is why I went into this field, so I could help kids process grief and trauma and give them healthy coping strategies."

They were silent. I strained to listen, my heart beating wildly. It couldn't be true. Emma's case *had* to be different. She had to still be alive. She just had to be.

"What happened?" I heard my mom's voice, and I tried to

calm myself down to listen again, inching down a couple steps, daring to get a little closer.

"The summer before my freshman year in high school, one of my best friends was kidnapped."

"Oh Molly, I'm so sorry. Did they—"

"Actually, I'd appreciate it if you could hold your questions until I'm done. It's a difficult story for me to tell, and I just need to get it out. Okay?"

"Yes, of course. Please go on."

"Two of my friends, Sharmel and Torrie, were walking on a country road in the middle of the day on a sunny Sunday afternoon in August. We lived in a small, rural town in Oregon. I mean tiny.

"At that time, in 1980, our town's population was only 2,386 people. It was a peaceful farming community, the kind where neighbors were friends and everyone knew each other. The only crime we had to speak of consisted of petty theft and occasional vandalism, very small-time stuff. It was a safe, idyllic place to raise a family.

"Anyway, Sharmel and Torrie were walking toward town when a white station wagon, with three men in it, pulled up next to them. The driver rolled down his window and asked for directions. He said they were from out of town and that they were lost.

"Sharmel, being the friendly, trusting, and sweet person she was, walked right up to the men in the car and began to tell them how to get to town. Suddenly, two of the men got out of the car, including the driver. He said he'd been driving since early morning and was tired; he wanted to switch drivers. Instead, the other man grabbed Sharmel, and the driver chased after Torrie.

"Torrie hadn't walked up to the car, so she was already four feet away. As soon as the guy headed toward her, she bolted. She got away because she ran track and was lightning fast. But Sharmel"—her voice wavered—"Sharmel wasn't so lucky." Dr. Sykes sniffed and audibly sighed.

She continued, "The two men forced Sharmel into their car, kicking and screaming. They sped off, and Torrie ran to the nearest neighbor's house. Later that day, a police hypnotist interviewed her, and she was able to give them most of the license plate number and a detailed description of the man who chased her.

"Two hours after Sharmel's abduction, the kidnappers allowed her to make a phone call from a pay phone at the Roselodge Market near Lincoln City.

"Her parents weren't home, so she called Torrie's mom. She was crying and she said, 'I'm hurting.' The kidnappers forced her to hang up the phone before she could get anything else out.

"That phone call was a huge breakthrough in the case. Within an hour, police and search teams dispatched to that market and the surrounding area. Before nightfall, they found a blue Nike tennis shoe on the beach, ten miles from the market where Sharmel had made the phone call. The shoe matched Torrie's description of the Nikes Sharmel had worn that day.

"It seemed like such a great lead. They were on the right trail. But the Oregon coastline is filled with countless tiny roads and forested land—the proverbial needle in a haystack.

"That was the last lead they had—for eleven days.

"For eleven excruciating days, the whole town hoped, prayed, and searched for her. For eleven days, we held vigils, clung to hope, and waited. Eleven days of not knowing where she was, not knowing if she was okay, or why they took her in the first place.

"On the eleventh day, a woman called the police. She claimed to be the sister of one of the suspects. She had seen his likeness on TV, from the police sketch they'd shown on the news. She said all three men were hiding at her house and she was sickened by what she'd learned. She turned them in.

"Within half an hour, the police were at the sister's house and the suspects were apprehended. But Sharmel? One of the thugs who'd taken her led the police to her in exchange for a lighter sentence. They found her lying in a ditch next to a dirt road in a heavily wooded area, an hour south of Lincoln City. She was dead.

"The bastards murdered her that first night. They'd said in their confessions that they were so hopped up on LSD that day that they got some crazy idea that it would be fun to grab a young teenage girl and . . ."

Dr. Sykes sobbed. Her mournful wails penetrated my soul. Silent tears trickled down my cheek as I cried, too. I cried for this poor girl who died thirty-five years ago. I cried for her family and friends who were robbed of having her in their lives, who didn't get to see her grow up. I cried for this girl who was the same age as Emma.

Dr. Sykes began speaking again. I didn't know if I could bring myself to hear anything more. But it was like a train wreck. I knew I shouldn't keep listening, but I just couldn't help myself.

"Those horrible monsters abducted, raped, and murdered my friend. They'd stabbed her to death. There were stab wounds on her back . . . and they'd slit her throat. Those vile creatures had ended Sharmel's life for no reason."

An eerie silence settled over the house. I thought about going into the living room to comfort her. I felt so sorry for Dr. Sykes, but I just didn't know what to do for her.

I stood up to go down there when I heard my mom say something. I stopped to listen, but I couldn't hear her. Her voice was so quiet it was nearly a whisper. I continued down but hesitated toward the bottom of the stairs, unsure what to do next. Then Dr. Sykes continued with her story.

"At that time, the death penalty was legal in Oregon, but it hadn't been used in eighteen years. Still, we were sure they'd execute the three psychos.

"But before the case went to trial, the Oregon Supreme Court unanimously ruled capital punishment unconstitutional. The judge had no choice but to give them life sentences.

"This news outraged our tiny town. Many of the moms marched on the steps of the capitol building in Salem. They had signed petitions. They were able to get capital punishment reinstated.

"But it was too late. The trials were over. Sharmel's killers were given life with the possibility of parole. I can't even imagine that any of them could ever be released, could ever be free . . . ."

Her words trailed off and I had trouble hearing her. She spoke so quietly. I felt bad for eavesdropping, but I just couldn't stop. I strained to listen.

". . . I heard one of them was lit on fire when another prisoner threw a fire bomb into his prison cell, but he survived. Perhaps that was some kind of karmic justice, I don't know.

"But my friend? She's gone forever. Her innocence and life taken, cut short, with no rhyme or reason to it. We never got to say goodbye.

"And if that's not tragic enough, we were never given a chance to mourn and grieve properly. To heal. We were discouraged from talking about it. No one knew how to handle it, how to process our feelings, so the whole town just clammed up. Everyone tried to move on with their lives and go back to normal.

"But there would never be a normal for us. For Sharmel's class. Teachers and administrators pretended it hadn't happened. Here we were, entering high school for the first time . . . a time already fraught with anticipation, dread, and excitement. Yet, for us, there was this enormous, impenetrable dark cloud. It hung in the air, sucking out all the joy.

"We were overwhelmed with the unspeakable tragedy of Sharmel's abduction and brutal murder. We were in shock that such horrendous evil could exist in the world, much less our idyllic tiny town. We all had collective PTSD.

"There were no grief counselors back then. We couldn't talk about it. The administration was in such a hurry to move on, they neglected to honor her memory, her life. By 'forgetting it ever happened,' they were forgetting Sharmel. They were doing her a huge disservice. By not allowing us to talk about what happened to her, we also stopped talking *about her*.

"I became a psychologist so I could help kids deal with their feelings. I want to help teens process grief, and the tragedies that happen in their lives, in a healthy way—not to stuff it down like I had to. I wanted to honor my friend's life. I wanted to keep the good memories about her alive. Her voice was silenced too soon, but she has not been forgotten."

"Tell me about her. What was she like?" Mom encouraged.

"Sharmel was kind to everyone she met, a champion of lost souls and the friendless. She was a softball player, a cheerleader, a co-lead in the eighth-grade school play. She had many friends and was popular—adored by students, teachers, and the community. She attended church with her family every Sunday and was active in her church's youth group.

"Her joy and zest for life were infectious. She needs to be

remembered. How was such a vibrant life like hers snuffed out so early? Before she had a chance to live?

"I want to help kids deal with these losses. And right now, I'm afraid V has lost Emma."

My feet raced down the remaining few steps and I burst in on them before my mind could catch up. I shouted and cried inconsolably. "I'm really sorry about what happened to your friend. Truly, I am. But you're wrong! Emma is alive! I know she is! You're wrong! And you need to leave now. You're upsetting my mom."

Mom and Dr. Sykes shot up off the couch and stared at me. I must have startled them.

"V!" Mom warned, her tear-soaked eyes blazing into me.

"Mom, the doctor said you can't be under stress. Remember? Dr. Sykes is wearing you out." I turned to direct my gaze at her. "Please go now."

"What doctor? Hannah, what's wrong? What's going on?" Dr. Sykes looked confused.

"That's enough, V. We're not telling people yet, remember?"

"Oh!" I covered my mouth with my hands. "I didn't realize. I mean . . . um."

"Hannah? What's going on?" Dr. Sykes repeated, clearly not going anywhere.

Mom sighed. "Molly, I'm afraid I received some rather unpleasant news about my health last week. Perhaps you'd better sit back down."

IO
WE ARE WARRIORS

Even though Dr. Sykes agreed not to tell anyone, Mom told her employer. She'd already had her first chemo session and to take a sick day. They had also warned her that her hair would fall out soon, so she figured she might as well rip the Band-Aid off now and tell the principal about her cancer diagnosis.

By ten o'clock Thursday morning, word that my mom had breast cancer had spread all over the school. Former students poured into her classroom in droves to offer their sympathy, homemade cards, and words of encouragement.

Two seniors, former students, created a 'You caring' account for her; it's a charitable crowdfunding campaign. One student had lost a grandparent to cancer. He knew the treatments were expensive, too expensive for two teachers' salaries, and that insurance wouldn't cover all the costs.

Rebecca Nichols, Mom's best friend, created an account on Caring Bridge, a personal health website. It was like a blog, so Mom could update everyone online all at once. By keeping a health journal of news and updates to share with friends and family, she'd stop the influx of phone calls and well-wishers asking for information.

Once people knew, stuff happened crazy fast. When we got to school the next morning, a sea of pink greeted us in the quad. Students and staff wore pink shirts to show their love and support. There were hundreds of students—and school didn't start for another thirty minutes—unless you count zero period, but who in their right mind would want to come to school an hour early every day to go to another class? *Not me.*

Dr. Fitz stood at the top of the steps, an area that was sometimes used as a stage for announcements during break and lunch. It led down into the quad, an open area in the middle of campus with tables, chairs, and benches. It was basically an outdoor cafeteria. Giant speakers stood at each end of the stage, complete with a PA system. This was an organized ambush!

Dr. Fitz motioned for Mom to join him at the top of the steps. Four students stood with him to present her with a gift, an oversized glass jar filled with hundreds of encouraging notes.

Dad and I helped Mom navigate through the pink mob to get her to the stage, then we stopped at the bottom. We watched Mom climb the six steps to the top, take the microphone from Dr. Fitz, and turn toward her audience. A hush fell over the crowd.

She was overcome with emotion. I could see tears forming in her eyes. Yet, when she spoke, her voice was clear. I looked around and saw that every eye was on my mom. Not one kid looked at their phone, and no one took pictures or tried to record it, out of respect. I choked up as the realization hit me how much everyone admired my mom. I was overcome, too. I tiptoed away from the steps as quietly as I could and shrunk back into the crowd. I did not want anyone to notice me blubbering like an idiot.

"A big, giant THANK YOU to all of you from the bottom of my heart. I have never felt so loved in all of my life. I am simply in awe. Your love and support mean so much. You have given me strength. I feel like my heart will explode. Your love, your kind words . . . thank you. I love you all beyond reason. I will win this fight for EVERYONE!"

Thunderous applause and cheers resounded throughout the crowd. Students gathered around my mom for hugs, high fives, and fist bumps. Dr. Fitz said a few kind words, then dismissed everyone to head to their morning classes.

Mom was in her element. The more the spotlight shined on her, the more radiant she became. It was as if every card, note, text, call, word, thought, and prayer truly did strengthen her. She became an advocate for the cause—for a cure.

She wrote her first public message, a Facebook post to over two thousand adoring fans, which consisted mainly of the many former students and parents whose lives she'd touched over the years. Dad and I didn't want to read it. We didn't want to be in the spotlight, limelight, or any other light. Besides, my dad and I didn't have a Facebook account, anyway. We weren't sure why Mom was so open and public with such a personal, private health matter, but she was. We could fight it or embrace it. Well, at least the free meals were nice.

But it didn't stop with just meals. There was an outpouring of generosity, from meals and donations, cards and flowers, to student alumni with powerful connections, which all snowballed and took on a life of its own. Mom ended up with the best oncologist, specialists, nurses, and care possible. Her diagnosis became all-consuming, completely taking over our lives. My life.

The next day at school, students wore black t-shirts with pink writing that said, "FIGHT STRONG Like A Warrior," in honor of my mom. A kid I didn't know walked up to me, hugged me, and handed me a t-shirt.

Dr. Sykes called me into her office and asked if I'd read my mom's Facebook post.

"No, I don't have Facebook," I said, not wanting to look at her.

"I think you should read it," Dr. Sykes said.

"Like I said, I don't have Facebook."

She reached into her top desk drawer and pulled out her phone. She opened an app, scrolled through it, and held out her phone toward me. "V, I really think you should read this. I know you're hurting and you want to find Emma, but your mom is hurting, too. She needs you right now."

"My dad didn't read it either," I shot back, refusing to budge.

She held the phone out, unfazed. *Stalemate.*

I sighed and finally took the phone out of her hand. I looked at the screen and read the post. As I read, a single tear slid down my cheek. The one, try as I might, I couldn't hold in. I knew Dr. Sykes was watching me, waiting for the dam to burst, waiting for me to crack. I couldn't do it. Not in front of her. Now was not the time to fall apart. I still needed to find Emma.

Mom's Facebook post, **if you want to read it, is as follows:**

I like sunlight on everything, so please feel free to share this with friends and family—the more people affected by what we do, the better. And I want to make an impact in every sense.

In summary, Carlos and I found out on September 3rd that I have stage four breast cancer ... a shock to our world. I have started chemotherapy, which will be followed by radiation and surgery, and then hormone therapy (estrogen positive). From what I gather, my future will involve clinical trials. I will embrace science, research, love, prayer, and even some weird alternative stuff. And if that isn't enough, my husband of nearly 16 years, my fierce knight-in-shining-armor who would take on the entire universe for me, let alone a mutated cell ... he is a rock. He has never, he will never, and he is unable to ever give up on me. It is our fight. Carlos is at my side and in my heart through every single second of this challenge. He is the strongest, most wonderful man I have ever known. He is also notoriously private, which is why he probably shouldn't read my posts.

I've never had such a clear purpose or felt so loved. The outpouring of support has soaked us with strength. It is BEAUTIFUL. I am more present than I have ever been. I fall in love with people and life on a daily basis. I didn't think it was possible for me to love Carlos more, but somehow I do. And pink Friday! It was one of the most beautiful moments of my existence. I will hold it with me as I fight. I am taping up the quad photo of you all, the "sea of pink" in my house where I can see it every single day. I love it!

Ironically, one of the challenges for us has been in accepting financial help. It takes some very sincere humility and we are gradually coming to terms with it. We were told that it would happen with or without our consent (students and their parents, family, neighbors, friends, relatives, the community—all VERY stubborn). So we have kept an open mind, especially at the urging of people we know who have fought cancer themselves or with a child. They have told us of the financial burdens.

We want to be abundantly CLEAR on this point though ... we hope we don't have to use a dime. We hope to direct it to people who are in even more need, to research, to funding clinical trials, to anything that will wipe cancer's mutated genetic code off this Earth. From what I understand, my future involves clinical trials, perhaps for a very long time. We know there will be certain medications not covered by our insurance. Sometimes the research process and the FDA are just too slow for someone with my diagnosis.

In the meantime, it gives us such an incredible peace of mind to know that if these expenses come up, we will be okay. We don't know how we can possibly thank or repay our friends, family, neighbors, and fellow teachers at Sierra. We are truly astounded by the breathtaking outreach. The beauty of every gesture, kindness, and goodwill you have given our family is beyond comprehension. Your love, your words, your ridiculously generous financial contributions to our family's well-being and fight against cancer, are astounding. I have cried more in the last 10 days for joy than for anything else, and it is because of you. THANK YOU. I will be here for a long time! I will win this fight.

Please understand that we plan on paying everything forward, no matter how long it takes. I want to give back the beauty you have given me and my family through this, to give back to every single person who has reached out to us. I love you all beyond all reason.

THANK YOU from our family,

Carlos, Hannah, Violet, and Scotty

MANY KIDS I didn't know waved at me in the halls, or smiled, or nodded, or worse . . . gave me the pity stare.

It was too much. In one week, I had gone from being invisible to 'the kid whose mom has cancer.' And not just any mom —my mom. And my mom just happened to be the most popular teacher on campus. And my mom happened to have a big mouth and broadcast her life all over the school, our town, and the Internet. I didn't ask for this. And I definitely didn't sign her Facebook post. Why did she have to tell the world? I wanted to scream.

II
SOCCER PRO

Dr. Sykes called me into her office—again.

"We have to stop meeting like this," I groaned as I plopped down into the chair in front of her desk.

"V, I'm concerned about you." She pushed a box of Kleenex toward me.

Subtlety is not her best attribute.

I nearly laughed but caught myself in time. "Of course you are. It's your job, isn't it?"

Ignoring my snarkiness, she continued, "I'm concerned that all the extra attention you're getting, due to your mother's announcement last week, is affecting you. Do you feel angry toward her for making your private family lives so transparent and public?"

"Gee, I don't know. What do you think, Doc?"

"V, I'm trying to help you. Again, I can't help you if you won't talk to me."

"And *again*, I don't need your help! I'm fine. Stop worrying about me and help me find Emma. If you really want to help me so bad, that's what you can do for me—*find Emma!*"

"V, I think you're using Emma's abduction to distract you from what's going on with your mom. I think you need to face the reality that—"

"Don't say it! Don't you dare say it. I swear . . ." My eyes glistened, tears threatening to spill over onto my cheeks.

Softer, like she was talking to a child, she continued, "I know you've been through a lot lately, V . . . more than anyone your age should ever have to handle. It's okay to cry. It's okay to be upset. I'm here for you. We need to come up with coping skills for you to accept and manage your grief. It's been two weeks, and I think it's time for you to accept that Emma isn't coming back . . . so that you can mourn her loss, so you can heal and move on."

I stood up and glared at her, wiped the tears and snot off my face with my sleeve and said, "Yes, I'm upset. But I don't need to 'manage' my grief because EMMA'S NOT DEAD! I need you to stop saying she is. I'm upset because you won't get off my back. Now leave me alone and let me find my friend."

I raced out of her office, down the hall, and out the double doors. And then I ran some more. I just kept running.

ABOUT A MILE LATER, I had to stop. When I looked around, I realized I was in front of a park. I walked slowly to a bench and dropped down on it, relief enveloping me. While still gasping for air, I grabbed my sides and bent over in pain.

The problem is, I'm not a runner. I don't have an athletic bone in my body. I had asthma as a kid and never learned to play any sports. I'm just a skinny, scrawny 14-year-old who still resembles an 11-year-old. Seriously. I'm not sure I've even hit puberty yet. I barely have any boobs (if you can even call my tiny bumps boobs) and I haven't got my period yet. I'm what my mom calls a "late bloomer."

Emma, however, got her period last year during a soccer game. She was mortified. She'd had to run off the field when a player from the other team pointed at her, laughing, and said, "You've got blood on your butt!"

She'd locked herself in the bathroom stall in the girl's locker room and wouldn't come out until I came to the rescue with a feminine pad and some clean clothes. And that was the only time she'd ever walked off the field. Emma has played club soccer since she was six.

In fact, it's a wonder we're friends sometimes. Emma is a natural-born athlete and is good at everything she does. Soccer is her passion, and that's putting it mildly. Emma lives for soccer. She has posters of Mia Hamm, two-time Olympic gold medalist and two-time FIFA Women's World Cup champion, on display all over the walls of her bedroom.

Emma could play any sport she wanted to if she put her mind to it—she's that good. Her mom and grandma are super proud of her and go to all her games. Of course, they're hoping she gets a scholarship to a prestigious college. And who knows? Maybe she will. Maybe she'll even go pro someday. At least, that's her dream.

She knows her mom can't afford to send her to college. And Emma's dad—her hero—a great soccer player himself in his youth, is tragically not a part of her life.

Her father, Máximo Moreno, was born in Durango, Mexico. He immigrated to the States with his family at age 12, met

Emma's mom, Rosa, when they were both 16, and married at 18. Baby Emma was born two years later.

Máx fell in love with America and applied as soon as he could for U.S. citizenship. At last, he was an American citizen with a family, living the American dream. He was filled with pride for his new country.

When President Bush declared the War on Terror after the September 11 attacks in late 2001, Máx declared it his civic duty to fight for his country. He enlisted in the Army, was shipped off to Afghanistan, and was killed in action a few months later. Emma was still a baby.

Her dad died a hero, and all she has to show for it is a fancy medal and an American flag. The last time her father held her in his arms, she was only six months old. Her mom's heart remains broken. Rosa never remarried, so Emma is an only child.

Thinking about Emma like this made me even more determined to find her. I needed to step it up. I walked another mile to the police station. I had to know if they'd had any more leads or breaks in the case.

"Hello, V. What brings you in here in the middle of the day when you should be in school? Hmm?" Detective Lomeli towered over me.

At six-foot-two and muscular, Police Detective Andrew Lomeli was an intimidating man. He looked to be in his forties, African American, buzz-cut hair, no ring on his finger, no family photos on his desk, and he never smiled. He wore a crumpled brown suit with a thin black tie, and his black shoes needed a good polish. By the looks of him, I'd be willing to bet he'd never been married and most likely lived alone.

Ignoring his comment about school, I sat down next to his desk and waited for him to sit down, too.

He gazed at me for a beat, crossed and uncrossed his arms, then eventually sat down. "All right, what's on your mind, V?"

"What's going on with Emma's case? Have you found her kidnapper yet? What leads do you have? Did you find the gray SUV? Did you go back and talk to Mrs. Lee again? Maybe she remembers something she forgot to tell you before, something that could help you find Emma."

"First of all, do you have any idea how many gray SUVs are registered in the city of Orange? And we don't even know if the driver is local. He could live anywhere in Orange County—or even Los Angeles County, for that matter. Gray happens to be the most popular vehicle color in this area, and there are many shades of gray. That lead gave us nothing! And what could old, blind Mrs. Lee possibly still have to tell me that could help us find Emma?"

"I don't know. You're the cop! It's just that she's our only witness, and maybe she saw something else that she forgot to mention."

"V, what do you mean by 'our' witness? And how do you know her name, anyway? The press didn't release the name of the witness."

"I did a little investigating. It wasn't hard. I saw her house on a news report because the reporter was standing in front of it when he went on the air."

Lomeli furrowed his brow and cupped his hand over it as if he had a headache. "Child, please tell me you did not go over to Mrs. Lee's house and bother that poor ol' woman?"

"Don't call me child. And what if I did? It's a free country."

He laughed. "Well, that may be, but there are still laws about citizens pretending to be police officers and running around trying to solve crimes, getting in danger, and possibly getting their nosy selves killed."

"I didn't pretend to be a police officer!" I insisted, offended. But then I blurted out, "I pretended to be a reporter."

"Aha! So you did go over there. And impersonating a reporter is illegal, too, by the way."

"Is it?"

"It is if you forge IDs and press passes to get into places you don't otherwise have access to."

"I see. Good thing I didn't do any of those things. Now, about Emma. Why aren't you out there looking for her right now?"

"And just where do you suggest I look? Sorry, V, but I think it's time to admit your friend isn't coming back. It's already been two weeks, all our leads have dried up, and we need to face facts. Based on what we know from the way she was taken, we suspect that Emma may have already been murder—"

"Don't say it. And you're wrong. She's still alive. She's out there, and you're not looking for her. If you won't help me, I'll just find her myself! I'll never stop looking for her!" I got up and ran out of the station before Lomeli could say anything more to devastate me.

12
GLASS STARS

I was in my room when Mom and Dad got home. "V, could you come down here, please?"

Uh-oh. He's using his stern voice. My father rarely used his stern voice. I slowly descended the stairs, as I dreaded whatever punishment awaited me. "Hi, Dad! How was your day?" I plastered on a radiant smile.

"Cut it out, V. You know what you did."

"Um?"

"Oh, come on. Did you think we wouldn't find out? We work at your school, remember? What were you thinking, taking off like that? You stormed out of Dr. Sykes's office before lunch and played hooky the rest of the day!"

"I 'played hooky'? Wow, Dad. No one says that anymore."

"This isn't funny, young lady. There will be serious repercussions."

"Why won't she just leave me alone?"

"Nice try, but blaming Dr. Sykes isn't going to excuse the fact that you behaved irresponsibly, ditched classes, left campus, and had us all worried sick. You didn't call or text anyone. We had no way of knowing if you were dead or alive. What if the same guy who took Emma took you, too?"

"I wish he would. Then I could kick his ass and rescue her."

"V."

"Sorry, Dad. I didn't mean to worry you. I just needed to let off some steam, that's all."

"Where did you go?"

"To the police station to talk to Lomeli."

"What? Sweetie, you need to leave the police alone and let them do their job," Mom chimed in.

"Then they need to *do their job* and find Emma!"

Mom and Dad exchanged glances.

"What? What aren't you telling me? Is there news of Emma?" I was desperate to hear news, any news—except that they'd found her dead body.

"V, there is another reason we were worried about you today. We thought you might have heard about it somehow."

"Heard about what?"

"I got a call half an hour ago from Detective Lomeli. He had news to tell me, but he didn't mention anything about your little visit to him today, which I think is odd considering you skipped school and—"

"Dad! Stop stalling. What is it? Tell me. Please!"

"Another girl is missing. Lomeli called as a courtesy to let us know before we heard about it in the media. He called Rosa, too."

"Someone else has been kidnapped? Who—who is it?"

"We don't know if she's been kidnapped for sure."

"Dad."

"Brylee Rossi. Do you know her?"

"Brylee?" I slowly nodded. "Sort of. Brylee is in my Geometry class. She's older than me; 16, I think. I heard she flunked Algebra her freshman year and that's why she's just now taking Geometry. What do you mean she's 'missing'?"

"Well, they can't call it an abduction until they collect some evidence and hopefully find some witnesses. But I'm pretty sure she was taken. The detective said she stayed home from school today; she told her mom she was sick. She ended up going to the mall instead. Apparently, a little retail therapy was what she needed to get over her ailments."

"Carlos!" Mom scolded.

"Sorry, that was really insensitive. I didn't mean it; it's just that kids lie about—never mind, this isn't the time for a lecture. Anyway, two store employees at Forever 21 confirmed she was there around noon today, but no one has seen her since, and they've searched the mall. That was four hours ago. Her car is still at the mall, and she doesn't answer her phone. The police think she may have been taken in the parking lot."

"Did anybody see the suspect? Get the license plate number? Is it the same gray SUV? This could be the big break in Emma's case that we need to find her!" I could barely contain my excitement.

"V, a classmate of yours has possibly just been kidnapped and you think it's good news?" Mom was incredulous.

"No, of course not. Sorry, that did not come out right. But if there's a witness who can link the two kidnappings, and if they got the license plate number, then maybe—"

"Maybe we all just need to take a break for a minute and think of that poor girl's family," Mom said. "I'm glad you're home safe, but as you can see, it's dangerous out there. So do me a favor and stop trying to be a teen detective, okay? Please.

I've got enough on my plate right now without having to worry about you, too."

"I know. I'm sorry, Mom. I love you." I hugged my mom, and she held on a little too long. I squirmed, so she let me go.

"I love you, too, sweetie, more than you'll ever know. But this day has worn me out. I'm going upstairs to lay down for a bit. And somebody, please go get Scotty."

"Okay, V, here's the car keys," my dad said and pretended to reach into his jean pocket.

"Ha ha, very funny, Carlos. By 'somebody,' of course I meant you." Mom crossed her arms.

"Right, I'm the somebody. Got it. Just messing around, dear." Dad kissed Mom on the forehead. "See you in a bit."

"Hold on, Dad. I want to go with you," I said and followed him out to the car.

Once we were in the car, Dad eyed me warily. "Spill it."

"What do you mean?" I asked sweetly.

"Why did you want to come with me to pick up your brother?"

"No reason, I just felt bad for worrying you earlier today, and I wanted to do something nice to, you know, be a good daughter for a change."

"Hmm, I see." He seemed unconvinced, so when we got to Alex's house, I jumped out of the car and ran up to the front door, ready to be a good big sister, too.

Scotty and Alex answered the door together.

"V! I am so glad to see you!" Scotty threw his arms around me, and I picked him up. He wrapped his legs around me as if he'd never let me go. We waved goodbye to Alex, and I carried Scotty to the car. I peeled him off me and eased him onto the back seat.

"Why are you here, V? You never come with Mom or Dad to get me. Are you okay? Is everything okay?"

"Wow, I really haven't been a very good big sister lately, have I? Everything's fine, squirt. There's nothing to worry about. I just wanted to ride along with Dad for a change."

"Good. Because I don't want you to be sick, too . . . like Mommy. That would suck."

"Yes, it would indeed suck." I made sucking noises as I got in and shut my car door, and Scotty laughed.

My brother was a constant worrier. No one knows why or where he got it from. Perhaps it is in his genes. I mentioned he's adopted, right?

Scott Fitzgerald Jiménez was born six years ago in Vancouver, Washington, to Russian immigrant parents. Sadly, his mother died delivering him. Severely malnourished and too weak to push him out, she died moments after an emergency cesarean delivery.

Scotty's father, who had just lost his wife, didn't have a job and couldn't care for his newborn son. He also didn't speak English and wanted to go back to Russia. Not having any other family here, he did the only thing he knew to do. He put the baby up for adoption at an agency in Vancouver, which is a suburb of Portland just across the Oregon-Washington border.

My mom and dad had tried to have more children after me, but it wasn't working out for them. I didn't know all the details, but Mom's Aunt Karen, who worked at an adoption agency in Vancouver, finally talked them into adopting a baby. When Scotty was born, Mom had said "the stars aligned," and Aunt Karen had facilitated their adoption.

My parents had taken me to Grandma's and flown to Portland. A few days later, they'd come back with my eight-day-old baby brother. I was barely eight years old.

It had felt like my birthday all over again—with a new baby brother as my present! I got to hold tiny Scotty his first night with us while we watched the fireworks light up the night sky. I was instantly in love with the pale, blond little bundle.

But even then he had a worried expression on his face, like he couldn't relax because he had to brace himself for some impending inevitable doom. I wondered if he thought he was cursed, if he thought he'd killed his birth mother just by being born. I guess I'd go through life worried all the time, too.

"V, why aren't you answering me?" Scotty screamed.

"Sorry, what?" I realized we were still in the car.

"You never pay attention to me! I'm not saying it all over again because . . . well, because I forgot."

Dad and I laughed.

"It's not funny!" Scotty kicked the back of my seat.

"Hey, sorry little buddy. You're right. How about if I spend time with you tonight. I'll read you a bedtime story, just you and me, okay?"

"Promise?"

"Promise."

STILL WIDE AWAKE, Scotty lay in his bed and showed no signs of falling asleep any time soon. I helped him choose which pajamas to wear, we brushed his teeth, and we found his stuffed Minion under the bed. Then I got him a glass of water and read him two stories. *Now what?*

"Man, how does Mom do this every night?" I stared at him.

"Do what?" Scotty asked, staring right back.

"Get you to go to sleep?"

"She does the soft tickles."

"You mean she rubs your back?"

"Yeah, but with soft tickles."

"Do you want me to do the soft tickles?"

"Okay, but you have to do it like Mommy does."

"I'll try. Roll over, kid." I helped him push up his PJ top and lay down on the bed next to him, propped up on my side. I lightly let my fingertips rest on the back of his neck, then slowly tickled across his back, zigzagging down and then back up again. "How's that?"

"That's good!" Scotty said, clearly happy.

"You sound surprised."

"How did you know how to do it like Mommy?"

"Because she used to give me soft tickles, too, when I was your age."

"V, will you tell me about the glass stars?"

"Oh, I can't tell it like Mom. That's her story. She's the only one who can tell it right."

Scotty rolled back over, pulled his shirt down, and sat up. "Is Mommy going to break, like the glass stars in her story? Will she blow up into millions of pieces and turn into stardust?"

"No! Why would you think that? Mom's not a star."

"But she's fragile, like the glass stars. And Thunderbird's not here to rescue her."

"Scotty, where did you get that idea? She's not made of glass—"

"I heard Daddy say she was fragile, that we have to be careful with her because she's sick. And the glass stars are fragile, too; that's why they broke. And Thunderbird had to save them. But Thunderbird can't save Mommy!" He started to cry.

"Well, Dad didn't mean it like that. Besides, Thunderbird isn't real. That's just a story Mom made up that night, when we were stuck in the snow. There's no such thing as stars made out of glass. It was all pretend."

"Uh-uh! Thunderbird is too real!" Scotty cried even harder. "Don't say that, V!"

"What's this I hear about Thunderbird?" Mom came in and plopped down on the bed.

"Mommy, V says Thunderbird isn't real. She said there aren't really glass stars in the sky. But there are too! I saw them! Remember? I saw Thunderbird that night when we were in the snowy mountains. I did! But I don't want you to break, Mommy! Don't be fragile! Please, Mommy, don't break like the glass stars!" Scotty clung to our mom and buried his face in her hair, crying so hard he got the hiccups.

As Mom held and comforted Scotty, she looked up at me, her eyes glistening. "V, go get the magic hiccup cure, will you?"

"Sure, Mom." I grabbed Scotty's empty water glass off the nightstand and went down to the kitchen to refill it, adding a teaspoon of sugar, the 'magic' elixir to cure Scotty's hiccups. I was relieved to have been sent out of his room. I didn't know how Mom was going to handle his questions or clean up the mess I made by telling him the truth, but I knew I needed to get my own emotions under control before heading back in there.

As I neared Scotty's room, I took a couple deep breaths to prepare myself and listened at the door. To my surprise, Scotty's hiccups were gone, and he wasn't crying anymore. Instead, they were declaring their love for each other.

"I love you to the sun, the moon, and the stars!" Scotty said.

"And I love you to the stars and infinity—forever!" Mom said back.

"Tell me the story again, about the legend of the glass stars. Just one more time."

"Many moons ago, long before people inhabited the Earth,

there were only animals. Among them lived an enormous, giant bird. According to the Native American legends in these lands, this giant bird, who resembled an eagle, but was much, much bigger, was called Thunderbird . . ."

I decided to leave them alone and tiptoed away from Scotty's room, returning to my own.

13

RED RAIN

As I put the final touches on my essay, an assignment that was due last Friday, I heard a strange, muffled sound coming from Mom's room. I looked at the clock; it was 11:06 p.m. I got up, walked down the hall, and stopped to listen at her bedroom door. She was laughing, but this was not my mother's usual laugh. This laugh sounded maniacal.

I hesitated before I knocked on the door and asked, "Mom? Are you okay? Can I come in?"

"Just a second, V," she managed in between crazy laughter. Finally, the door opened and she stood there in her bathrobe. "Come on in. You're probably wondering what's so funny, right?"

"Something like that, yeah." I eyed her, trying to assess the situation.

"Well, the dreaded day is here. My hair has begun to fall out."

"Really? But why were you laughing?"

"Go look at my bathroom floor."

I did. I saw big red clumps of Mom's hair all over the white linoleum floor, sink, and counter. I didn't know what to say.

"It was a veritable red rainstorm. You should have seen it. When I turned on the hair dryer, wisps of strawberry tufts wafted all through the air. They swirled to and fro as they left my head and plunged to their demise. I laughed and cried at the same time. My hair is my trademark, after all."

"That's not true. Your hair is not you; it's just hair. You'll still be beautiful without it!"

"Thank you, sweetheart. I guess I needed to hear that."

"Mom?"

"Yes?"

"I'm sorry I messed things up with Scotty tonight. He just kept insisting that you were made of glass and that you're going to break and—"

"It's okay, sweetie. He worries—you know that—but he's fine now. Just let him have his stories; they comfort him. At least for now, okay?"

"Of course." I started to leave and thought of something else. "But Mom?"

"Yes, V? What is it?"

"I don't want you to break either." I quickly added, "Good night, I love you," and walked out of her room without waiting for a reply.

As I closed the door, I heard her say, "You're not getting rid of me that easy—I'm unbreakable! Love you, too, kid!"

THE NEXT DAY, I skipped school to go with Mom to her doctor appointment, and that night we had a haircutting and head-shaving party on the back patio for her. Her doctor told her it was time to go ahead and shave it all off, but before I talk about that, I want to tell you about the head-shaving party.

I got to go first. I cut the right side of her hair, and Scotty cut the left side. We had fun whacking away at Mom's locks of hair because there was no pressure to make it pretty. We knew Dad would shave it all off when we were done creating our wild hairdo for her. It was way more fun than the time I had cut my Barbie's hair when I was five. And Scotty loved it.

By the time we were done with our masterpiece, it was a short, uneven pixie cut. Mom looked like a cartoon character who had just stuck her finger in a light socket. Her hair, what was left of it, was spiky and stood out all over.

Then it was Dad's turn. Mom didn't trust us kids with the electric razor. Can't say I blame her. When Dad shaved her head, he sprinkled it with tiny kisses after each grazing sweep. It was tender and sweet, and I think Mom dug it because she kept smiling, then got all teary-eyed.

After we finished, I ran and brought out a hand mirror to hold out in front of her so she could admire her bald head.

"Well? What do you think?" I asked her.

"I'd love to say I have a finely shaped skull, but I don't. It looks so funny. From now on, I'll be donning scarves, hats, and wigs whenever I venture out in public. I guess I can't say I can rock the tough, bald-badass look, huh?"

"I still think you're beautiful, Mommy." Scotty climbed on her lap and hugged her.

"Me, too!" I piled on.

"Me, three!" Dad encircled us all with his long, outstretched arms. We took a collective deep breath and sighed, unsure of exactly what the future held for this beautiful, brave, bald woman that I was proud to call Mom.

14

BRYLEE ROSSI

As I sat in Geometry, I kept staring at Brylee's empty seat and replaying yesterday's newscast over and over in my mind. So, as I said earlier, I didn't go to school yesterday because I wanted to go to Mom's doctor appointment with her. I felt protective of her.

After I learned that her hair was falling out, it made it so much more real. My mom had *cancer*. I asked to go to her doctor appointment and meet her oncologist because I had questions: What did having cancer mean? Will my mom die? How did she get it? Why did she get it? Can she be cured? I needed to know my mom would get the best care possible. I needed answers to my questions.

While we waited in the lobby at Dr. Khatri's office, a TV mounted near the ceiling in front of us sprang to life with a special news report announcement "interrupting the regularly scheduled program."

Brylee's yearbook photo from last year filled the screen. I inhaled sharply at the unexpected image. It had been less than twenty-four hours since her disappearance.

I didn't notice before, but Brylee bore a resemblance to Emma. They both had long black hair, dark brown eyes, and caramel-colored skin. But Brylee's features were more pronounced, sharper. Plus, she was taller and curvier than Emma. She was also two years older. After some quick sleuthing (looking her up on social media), I found out that her family was from Argentina and quite wealthy.

Emma's features are softer and warmer. Brylee is pretty, but Emma exudes warmth, kindness, and beauty. Or maybe it was just me, biased and missing my best friend.

Shaking my head, I cleared the memories and focused again on the news report blaring above me, "Brylee Rossi was last seen getting into a navy blue Toyota Sienna minivan with an Asian male approximately five feet, five inches tall, 140 pounds, and in his mid-30s. The van has tinted windows and a UC Irvine decal on the back bumper. It is unclear whether Miss Rossi was forced into the van.

"According to Police Detective Andrew Lomeli, an eyewitness only got a partial read of the license plate, so they're not releasing that information at this time. In a statement to the press issued this morning, the detective said he does not believe this matter is related to the Emma Moreno kidnapping case."

The video cut to Detective Lomeli in front of a bunch of microphones with reporters asking rapid-fire questions about Emma.

"So far, only one witness has come forward with information about Emma Moreno's abduction. That witness described a young white male driving a gray Ford SUV. At this point in the investigation, I don't believe these two cases are connected. There just aren't enough similarities to link them together, or to the suspect or suspects. But we have not ruled out any possibilities. We are following every lead we have. Our mission is to get these two girls home safely and back to their families as soon as possible. That will be all for now. Thank you."

The reporter came back on, "Police are taking statements from all eyewitnesses who were at the mall yesterday, as well as anyone who may have seen a suspicious gray Ford SUV two weeks ago, in the city of Orange. If you have information about either of these two cases, you are encouraged to call the police hotline at 1-800-82—"

"Hannah Jiménez? Mrs. Jiménez?"

Mom and I both jumped. She stood up. "I'm Hannah."

"The doctor will see you now." The nurse smiled and ushered us through a door and down the hall. I looked over my shoulder one more time at the TV, but I couldn't hear or see anything clearly enough.

Dr. Khatri, Mom's oncologist, was very kind and did her best to answer my questions. "Unfortunately, there is no cure for cancer." She crossed over and sat down on a stool next to me. "When patients say they are 'cancer-free,' it means that their tumor didn't grow back after they finished their treatments. After a patient has had clear scans for a few years, we consider that patient in remission. A complete remission means there are no signs of the disease on any of the tests we run, like a CT or PET scan. Some people remain in remission for many, many years and go on to live happy, healthy lives."

"But if the tumor is gone, then isn't that a cure? Doesn't that mean the cancer is gone, too?" I asked.

"Not necessarily. We can't say the cancer is gone forever. Once someone has the diagnosis of, and has been treated for, cancer, even after surgery where the tumor has been removed, there is always a chance there are still cancer cells somewhere in the patient's body. That's why we have to do the chemotherapy and radiation. The treatments attack and shrink the tumor, but they also attack any other cancer cells to try to eradicate them from your mother's body."

"But how did she get these cancer cells in the first place? Why did a tumor grow inside her?"

"We don't know exactly. Sometimes it's hereditary, and sometimes there are environmental factors—"

"Environmental? You mean something she was exposed to in the environment caused her cancer?"

"There are carcinogens that are likely to contribute, but—"

"V, that's enough," Mom warned. "Leave the nice doctor alone. I'm sure she has other patients to visit. We can talk about this later."

"Here's a pamphlet that should help you understand this better, V," Dr. Khatri soothed. "It's for the families of cancer patients."

I took the pamphlet and tried to smile, but I just wasn't feeling it. I still had more questions, and my mom wouldn't let me ask them. I let out a loud sigh.

They ignored me. Dr. Khatri talked to Mom about her hair loss. She said it was normal and right on schedule. She encouraged Mom to go ahead and shave it all off, that it would be easier and less stressful than watching her hair fall out at a rapid rate and finding clumps of hair all over the house.

That's when I got the idea to have the shave party.

Afterward, Mom wore a shoulder-length red wig, a gift from Rebecca, to work. She got tons of compliments. To those who knew her, it was obvious it wasn't her own hair, but to strangers, it looked natural.

Now I'm in Geometry, staring at Brylee's empty seat. Mr. Goodenough is going on about Pythagorean equations relating the sides of a right triangle in a simple way, and I'm replaying yesterday's newscast over and over in my mind.

Why did Lomeli make a point of saying the two cases aren't connected? Is he trying to throw people off? I think they are connected. No, I KNOW they're connected! I mean—Brylee and Emma look alike! Didn't anybody notice that? I don't think it's a coincidence. I think Lomeli knows more than he's telling the press.

Where are they? Maybe they're together right now. Maybe the person who took them likes girls with long black hair? Maybe it's just a lonely person who lost their daughters or something and kidnapped Emma and Brylee to raise in their place?

My mind raced with the possibilities, but I blocked out anything too scary. I wouldn't let myself imagine anything bad or violent happening to them. They had to be unhurt; they just had to be. More determined than ever to find both of them, I had to come up with a plan.

Hmmm, what would Veronica Mars do next? She'd get up and leave because the bell just rang—duh.

15

FOREVER 21

I rode my bike to the mall after school. Probably not the safest thing to do, in hindsight, but desperate times call for desperate measures—and I was desperate to find Emma and Brylee alive!

I walked into Forever 21, the last store Brylee had been spotted in before she'd headed out to the parking lot, from what my dad said Lomeli told him. I walked up to the sales counter. The salesclerk at the register didn't acknowledge me, so I cleared my throat. "Excuse me?"

"Can I help you?" The ponytailed clerk didn't even glance up from her phone.

I took out my own phone, found Brylee's picture from an Instagram post, and held it out to her. "Have you seen this girl?"

Ponytail put her phone in her back pocket and sauntered over to me. She took my phone out of my hand and studied the photo on the screen. "Yeah, I remember her. She was here two days ago. The police came in here asking about her, too. Did something happen?"

My eyes opened wide in surprise. *How could she not know?* "You don't watch the news, do you?" I asked.

"No, why?" Ponytail asked, finally paying attention.

"We suspect she was kidnapped that day. This was the last place she was seen right before someone saw her in the parking lot. The witness watched her get into a minivan."

"So talk to the person who saw her get in the van." She handed my phone back to me. "I don't know anything. I just work here."

"I'd love to talk to that witness, but I don't know who it is. I thought if I could retrace her steps—that is, if you could tell me anything helpful, like where she went after here—maybe I could find the other witness. Maybe they work at the mall, too."

"Hmm, sorry. I'd like to help you, but I just don't think I can tell you anything."

"You saw her, though, right?"

"Yeah, I saw her."

"Did she buy anything? Did she have any other purchases or bags with her? How long was she in here? Did you see anybody talking to her?"

"No, she was alone, and she didn't have any bags. She seemed kind of upset, though. She bought a light blue sweater and left, like she was in a hurry. She only looked around for like two minutes."

"Thank you. See, that was very helpful."

"It was? How do you figure?"

"Well, you said she was in a hurry, alone, and upset. That tells me that after this store she planned to go straight to her car."

"It does? Oh, okay. Cool."

"Think about it. If you were shopping alone at the mall and

something or someone suddenly upset you, would you want to keep shopping?"

"No, I'd wanna go home and drown my sorrows in a pint of Häagen-Dazs ice cream," she admitted.

"Exactly. I think someone scared her or something and she just wanted to get out of here."

"Wow, you deduced all that from a light blue sweater purchase?" a guy said as he appeared at the counter and walked up next to Ponytail clerk. "What if she'd bought a red sweater? Would that have changed anything?" He glowered at me.

"Good one, Curt," Ponytail said and gushed at him.

I rolled my eyes and glared back at both of them.

"So who the hell are you, anyway? Sherlock Holmes?" He folded his arms across his chest, still scowling.

"I'm V. I'm a classmate of Brylee's, but I'm also helping investigate this case. Who are you?" I tried to act authoritative.

"I'm Curt, the store manager." Curt paused and looked me up and down. He suddenly laughed and added, "You? You're 'investigating' this case?" He waved his air quote fingers in my face. "Ha! What are you, 12?"

"No! I'm in high school. I'm a teenage detective and—"

"Save it, kid. I don't believe you. But I'll go ahead and tell you what I told the cops; I'm feeling generous today. I was just coming in for my shift when I saw Brylee in the parking lot. I recognized her from school because, well, she's hot. I didn't tell the cops that part, though. So, like I told them, I locked my car and heard scuffling, like someone was being half dragged. I looked up and saw Brylee get into a blue minivan with some Asian guy."

"You go to my high school, but you work here in the middle of the day?"

"No, Sherlock. I graduated last year."

"Oh, sorry." Quickly overcoming my embarrassment, I launched back into detective mode. "Did you get a good look at the guy with Brylee?"

"Yep. A real class act, that one. He wore skinny jeans and a white T-shirt. His hair was shaggy and greasy, and he had a scruffy patch on his chin, like he's tryin' to grow a beard or something. Oh, and he's way older, too—so gross. Definitely not Brylee's type, ya know?"

"Who is her type? You?"

"Yeah, maybe." Curt puffed out his chest. "Look, 'V, the detective' or whoever you are, I don't know what kind of trouble she's gotten herself into, but I can tell you that Brylee did not go willingly with that creep. He must have something on her."

"What do you mean? Like what?"

"Like, she would never get into a *minivan* with a greasy 30-year-old loser. She's smokin' hot and popular. She could have any guy she wants. Plus, she's super stuck up and rich. She'd never be caught dead in a minivan!"

I winced at the word 'dead.'

"Okay, thanks Curt. You've been helpful. I have some other leads to follow up on, so I'll be going now."

"Oh yeah? Like what?"

"I'd rather not disclose that information due to the sensitivity of the case."

"Sure, kid. Whatever."

As I walked out of the store, Curt hollered after me, "Go get 'em, Sherlock. I hope you find that greaseball who took Brylee and kick him in the 'nads for me if he hurt her."

I smiled and whispered to myself, "I intend to do just that."

I PEDALED HOME FURIOUSLY, knowing my parents would be mad at me for riding my bike to the mall. Luckily, they weren't home yet. I parked my bike in the garage and ran upstairs to my room.

When they walked in the front door five minutes later, I sat at my desk and pretended to be engrossed in my homework. Mom came upstairs to check on me, and I quickly hid my notes from my conversation with the Forever 21 employees. If what Curt said was true, I had to figure out why Brylee got in that van.

16

SUZIE DENTON

Most days, I ate lunch in the library. I hated sitting at the lunch tables because people stared at me. I got pity stares because I was the girl whose mom had cancer, or the girl whose best friend was kidnapped, or people just looked at me funny because I sat alone—by myself—a complete and total loser with zero friends. So, yeah, I avoided the cafeteria and the whole lunch social scene as often as possible.

There was a pretty strict policy against food in the library, but the librarian, Miss Paroo, adored my mom. Since they shared a fondness for literature, with my mom being an English teacher and all, Miss Paroo practically thought my mom walked on water. Lucky for me, she extended her good-will toward me just for being my mother's offspring. Therefore, she let me bring food in as long as I was discreet about it and cleaned up any messes. I usually kept a peanut butter and jelly sandwich in my backpack and broke off little chunks of it to eat behind a book I'd sometimes pretend to read.

The best part about the library was that nobody stared at

me. In fact, no one even noticed me. Most students in there during lunch were cramming for a test or doing last-minute homework, so they definitely weren't looking around.

Anyway, I'd gotten used to the solitude and actually looked forward to my lunches in the library. Sometimes I'd even chat with Miss Paroo a bit, just to keep on her good side since she was breaking the rules for me.

That Friday, I sat in an alcove like usual, which felt like my own personal book nook because it was in the nonfiction section and hardly anybody ever went over there. I sat on a long, built-in-the-wall bench, hiding my peanut butter and banana sandwich behind a paperback copy of *Lord of the Flies*. I was still reading the book that Mrs. Nichols had assigned over two weeks ago. The test was coming up, and I had let myself fall behind. But with Mom's cancer and Emma's being kidnapped, it was sort of a free pass to not do my homework. All my teachers told me I could turn stuff in whenever. There was a perk in all of this after all, but not much of a silver lining, if you ask me. After all, I still had to make up the assignments eventually.

Anyway, as I sat there reading about boys gone wild, a girl I'd never seen before sat down next to me. Naturally, I ignored her and pretended I was engrossed in the best book ever. I slid my half-eaten sandwich down and behind my back.

She cleared her throat and moved closer.

I peered over the top of my book at her and blinked. She wore a black SHS hooded sweatshirt even though it was ninety degrees outside. She had mousy brown shoulder-length hair and wore glasses.

"Hi, V. My name is Suzie Denton. I'm a junior here, and I know all about your missing friend, Emma. I have something very important to tell you about her." She stopped suddenly.

Is she waiting for me to give her permission to speak? What a weirdo. What could she possibly know about Emma that I don't?

"Okay?" I waved her on.

"Not here," Suzie whispered.

"Why not here?"

"I don't want anyone to hear us."

"Okay then . . . where?"

"Meet me in the Chem Lab after school."

"But I have to go home with my parents after school."

"They have a meeting with Dr. Fitz after school today. You'll have time."

"How do you know that?"

"I'm an office aide fourth period. I heard Dr. Fitz on the phone with your mom."

Just then, my phone buzzed. It was a text from Mom.

"Dad and I have to meet with Fitz after school. It's probably just insurance stuff or planning for when I'll need a sub later. We shouldn't be long. Wait for us, okay?"

"*OK*," I texted back.

"All right, Suzie. You have my attention. Why the Chem Lab?"

"I know for a fact it will be empty, and I have a key."

"Why do you—"

"I'll tell you later. Just meet me there as soon as the bell rings, got it?"

"Yeah. Sure. See you—" She left before I finished my sentence.

* ★ ★ ★ *

I WAITED by the door to the Chem Lab for what seemed like an eternity but in reality was probably less than five minutes. Finally, Suzie appeared, produced a key, and let us in.

"What took you so long?" I whined. "I don't have much time, so let's make this quick, okay? My parents will be done with their meeting with Fitz soon. So why all the secrecy? What do you—"

"I live on Cedar Avenue." Suzie cut me off, then stared at me expectantly, waiting.

"What?" She had my attention as I tried to process what this could mean.

"I saw Emma get kidnapped," she said.

"WHAT? Why didn't you come forward? Why didn't you tell the police? Emma's been gone eighteen days and you waited until now to say anything? Are you kidding me? They only have one witness. And Lomel—er, the police think she's not a credible witness because she's old, blind, and doesn't speak English very well. What do you know? Tell me everything!"

"I would if you'd ever stop talking."

"Sorry." I bit my bottom lip to keep from shouting at her.

"I live two houses down from Mrs. Lee but across the street, so I had a different view—a closer view. My house is directly across the street from where Emma was taken.

"I heard a scream and immediately looked out the window, but I couldn't see anyone because they were on the other side of the van."

"You mean the SUV."

"No—it was a navy blue minivan."

"Wait, I don't understand. Emma was taken in a gray Ford SUV."

"Was she?"

"Suzie, what are you saying?"

"Let me finish. I didn't say anything until now because all I saw was a dark blue minivan. No license plates. No people. Not much to tell. And when I watched the news, they said they were looking for a gray Ford SUV. I figured I must not have witnessed Emma's kidnapping after all. What I saw couldn't have been the kidnapper's car, the scream I heard couldn't have been Emma, and I was wrong. I basically forgot about it, until now."

"But you heard a girl scream. Didn't that mean anything to you?"

"Maybe it was just a kid throwing a tantrum and not wanting to go to the first day of school. I don't know. I just tried to put it out of my mind because it was the wrong car.

"But then yesterday I heard about Brylee, that she left with an Asian man in a blue minivan, and I got chills. This is not a coincidence—it has to be the same van!"

I stared at Suzie, my heart racing wildly. In my gut, I knew she was right. Something clicked, and I just knew. I couldn't think clearly. Adrenaline coursed through my body as I was filled with new hope of finding Emma.

"If that's true, why would Mrs. Lee say it was a gray Ford SUV? It doesn't make any sense. She said she saw the whole thing. She may be blind, but she's not *that* blind."

"Maybe she lied." Suzie shrugged.

"What are you talking about? Why would she do that?"

"I think the Asian man who kidnapped Brylee is Mrs. Lee's grandson."

"WHAT?"

"I saw a composite drawing of him on the news. It looks just like Mrs. Lee's grandson—shaggy hair, scruffy beard. I've seen him mow her yard a few times."

"We have to tell the police! This is huge!"

"V, you need to calm down. You're not thinking clearly. Who's gonna believe a couple teenagers over Mrs. Lee?"

"You're right. We can't report this. If we do, it will be on the news, and it will tip her off."

"Her?" Suzie asked.

"You see it, right? Mrs. Lee has to be in on it."

"That sweet old woman? Are you crazy? I think her grandson is doing this on his own."

"But you're the one who said she lied," I reminded her.

"Well, yeah, I think she might be protecting her grandson, the kidnapper, but I don't think she has anything to do with the actual kidnappings. She's just an innocent old lady with a bad apple for a grandson."

"Well, there's one way to find out."

"I don't like the sound of that, V."

"We're going to spy on them."

"I was afraid you were going to say that. I hear you're trying to be some big teen detective and you're going to solve this case."

"I am!" I shouted.

"Shhh, keep your voice down. I have this key because I'm a teacher's aide for Chem, but we're not supposed to be in here after school. Do you want me to get in trouble?" Suzie glared at me.

"Sorry," I whispered. "But I can't contain my excitement. You just gave me my first big break." I wanted to hug her.

"I did? Um, that's great, but I'm not spying on anybody."

I ignored her and began thinking out loud, "The fact that the kidnapper took Brylee in the same minivan two weeks after taking Emma means he thinks that no one is onto him. He thought he was in the clear because Mrs. Lee made sure the cops were chasing a gray Ford SUV. But now he has to be more careful because of the Forever 21 witness who saw Brylee get in the blue minivan at the mall. I knew these were connected!

"Come on, Suzie. You can be my Wallace. Are you in?"

"Your who? No, I told you I'm not spying on anybody."

"You know, Wallace Fennel, Veronica's assistant. He helped her solve cases."

"Veronica who?"

"Haven't you ever seen *Veronica Mars* before? You know, the TV show?"

"Nope, I don't watch TV."

"Oh. Really?" I shook my head. "Well, never mind. Anyway, where's your sense of loyalty to Emma and Brylee? You want to find them, don't you?"

"I want the police to find them."

"Then why did you tell me all this? You secretly want to help me find them; you just don't know it yet. Come on, it'll be fun."

Suzie shook her head and said, "We can argue over this later. We better leave before the janitor comes."

17

STAKEOUT

I wanted to stake out Mrs. Lee's house with Suzie over the weekend, but she had to go out of town with her family. I had planned to go over there anyway, without Suzie. But one of my dad's teacher's pets saw me at the mall the day before and ratted me out. I was put on house arrest all weekend and forbidden to ride my bike. Ugh.

The weekend seemed to drag on endlessly. While pretending to catch up on homework, thus being allowed to stay in my room uninterrupted and excused from chores, I came up with a plan for how Suzie and I would catch Mrs. Lee. Or at least figure out what she knew. I wasn't convinced yet of her guilt. Maybe she really did have faulty eyes, or she was color blind, or senile?

But I knew deep down that simply wasn't true. I couldn't deny that she lied about the kidnapper's car. So what else did she lie about? Was her grandson really the kidnapper? Did she have something to do with this? She seemed like such a sweet old lady; it was hard to imagine. But then again, I never imagined Emma would get kidnapped or my mom would get cancer, either. My life was nothing like I imagined. Therefore, I had to keep an open mind and not rule out any possibilities.

Tuesday would be Mom's second chemo treatment. I figured I could sneak out then and go to Mrs. Lee's house after school with Suzie. In the meantime, I had to stay under the radar and attract the least amount of attention possible. If Mom and Dad forgot about me, maybe they'd forget I was grounded, too. By pretending to be buried under copious amounts of homework (Who was I kidding? I really did have a ton of homework! But I obviously had other priorities—like finding my best friend!), my parents wouldn't suspect me of being up to anything, and they'd be more likely to leave me alone.

Saturday was Scotty's first soccer match. Mom's doctors continually advised her to keep life as normal as possible, to fill it with activities and routines. By keeping busy, we kept our minds off Mom's disease and focused on 'healthy' things.

Yeah right. Focusing on Emma's kidnapping is far from healthy. But getting her back? That would be awesome.

So, they signed Scotty up for soccer right away. They'd talked Alex's parents into signing him up, too, which thrilled Scotty.

Scotty had always known he was adopted. It was just a fact, much like the facts that he had blond hair and blue eyes. He knew Mom and Dad loved him. He knew he belonged in our family, but he was also proud of his Russian heritage. When he signed up for soccer, he loved correcting his new teammates.

"Did you know that soccer is really called football in Russia? Did you know football is the number-one sport in Russia? And even in the world? Did you know I'm Russian?"

And so it went. Dad said they lost their first match, one to zero. Scotty was unfazed. "That's okay. We'll get 'em next time!"

I got out of going to Scotty's match by playing the homework card. The truth was, I just didn't want to go to a stupid soccer game with a bunch of six-year-olds running all over the field with no clue as to where the ball even was, let alone the goal. I had to figure out how Suzie and I were going to catch Mrs. Lee without getting caught ourselves.

THE REST OF THE WEEKEND, and Monday, creeped along like a snail going uphill on hot asphalt in the middle of a summer day. By Tuesday, I had everything I needed.

Since Mom had her chemo treatment later that morning, I talked her into letting me ride my bike to school. The kidnappings, and my tendency to wander off without permission, made Mom and Dad super strict for the first time. I wasn't used to having so many rules, or my freedom squashed. I didn't like it at all and rebelled every chance I got. I still had a case to solve, which no one seemed to understand.

After school, I rode my bike to Suzie's house, and we put 'Operation Spy on Mrs. Lee' into action.

I grabbed my notebook out of my backpack and thrust it into Suzie's hands. "These are my notes. I compared what Mrs. Lee told the police with what Curt, the Forever 21 manager, told them. With your also seeing the blue van, and what we learn today, we should have enough information to go to the police so they can arrest Mrs. Lee and her grandson—and we can find Emma and Brylee!"

"I don't know. What makes you think the police will listen to us?" Suzie picked at her fingernails, not making eye contact with me.

"Because we're telling the truth. Truth and justice shall

prevail. Don't be nervous about it. I'll coach you." I cleared my throat dramatically. "Now, let's go over what we know."

Suzie and I sat side by side on her bed and studied the notes sprawled out before us. On one sheet, I'd made two columns:

The Witness Reports

Mrs. Lee saw	Curt saw
White male	Asian male
young, 20s	30s
short blond hair	shaggy black hair
clean-shaven	scruffy beard
thick build	skinny
5'10"	5'5"
red baseball cap	no cap
black T-shirt	white T-shirt
sagging jeans	skinny jeans
gray Ford SUV	navy blue Toyota Sienna minivan with UCI sticker

"The only common element these two witness reports share is that the suspect is male," I said. "If you hadn't told me it was really a blue minivan and not a gray SUV that snatched Emma, I would have thought these were two different suspects. And if it really is Mrs. Lee's grandson, then she must know what he's done, which is why she made up a totally different description to throw off the cops. Plus, when people lie, they tend to pick opposites. It's involuntary."

"What do you mean?"

"Have you ever played a word association game? You know, like, what's the first thing that comes to mind when I say the word '*cat*'?"

"Dog!" She laughed. "Oh wow, I guess you're right."

"Yep. Notice every description is its opposite: short blond hair vs. shaggy black hair, black T-shirt vs. white T-shirt, et cetera."

"Okay, so that makes sense why the descriptions of the two suspects are so different."

"One suspect," I corrected her.

"Hmm, okay." Suzie paused. "Let me think about this for a second." She stood up and walked over to her bedroom window, which faced Mrs. Lee's house across the street. She gazed out at the spot where she'd seen the van three weeks ago. "If I saw Emma get taken, and I'm 99 percent sure I did, then it's the same blue van and suspect who took Brylee. But I didn't actually see the guy—or Emma. I only heard her scream. Still, I saw the blue van, and I watched it drive away fast—the guy peeled out. It just has to be the same kidnapper."

"I agree, and that links the two cases. Both cases have the

same method of operation: snatch the girl, make her get in the minivan, and peel out fast. Everything and nothing makes sense. We're dealing with one suspect and two kidnappings. But why?"

"And if it's true, why would Mrs. Lee call the police at all? Why not just stay out of it? She proactively called 911 and filed a police report. She intentionally gave them false information to throw them off. I don't get it."

"Yeah, it's pretty risky. She has to be in on it! She went out of her way to cover this up, so she must have a reason. She must have assumed no one witnessed Emma get taken, that no one would contradict her story, so she could throw the police off her trail and tell them whatever she wanted. Thank goodness you saw something, Suzie!"

"I know. I only wish I'd told you sooner."

"Don't beat yourself up about it. Like you said, you didn't know for sure until you saw the news report after Brylee had been taken." I stopped and shook my head.

"What?" Suzie's eyes grew wide.

"It's making more sense now. I remember that Mrs. Lee went out of her way to tell me the guy wore 'sagging jeans.' She said they were like the kind the 'gang kids' wear. The best lies are the ones told in detail. The details make them more convincing. And, if she's so blind, how would she be able to tell if the guy's jeans were baggy or not? Especially if it happened so fast, like she said?"

"Good point."

"Okay, are you ready to do this?"

Suzie furrowed her brow but nodded with a slight lowering of her chin.

I took it as a green light and burst into action, excited for the next step. I jumped up and grabbed my backpack, dumping its contents out onto Suzie's bed. I looked up at her with a grin wider than the Cheshire cat.

"Whoa! Where'd you get all this cool spy gear?"

"You'd be surprised what your mom's credit card, an eBay account, and rush shipping can get you. The Internet is a beautiful thing. I ordered this Saturday, from the comfort of my laptop, and—voila!"

On the bed was an amplifier with a microphone and headphones, a bugging device and audio transmitter, and a small recorder. I picked up the amplifier. "This is an extreme sound amplifier. It's a listening device with a highly sensitive microphone that will even pick up a whisper. But we have to take turns listening because it only works with one set of headphones."

"Cool! Will it work from my bedroom? Can we just open the window and point it at Mrs. Lee's house?"

"I thought about that. It has a range of 300 feet, which is almost the length of a football field, but it will pick up *every* sound between your house and Mrs. Lee's. Plus, I don't think it goes through walls. We have to hope there's an open window or something."

"So, what do you think we should do?"

"We have to park your mom's car in front of Mrs. Lee's house. We can crack the window and slump down so it looks like the car is empty. We can listen from there."

"No way! You're crazy. That's too close—Mrs. Lee will catch us."

"Do you want to help me catch Emma's kidnappers or not? You're either with me or—"

"Of course I do! But—"

"But nothing. You do have your mom's car keys, right?"

"Yeah, she lets me drive it to school every day. But if I want to go anywhere else, I have to ask first."

"We're not *going* anywhere. You're just reparking her car across the street. No big deal. Where is your mom, anyway? Will she be home soon?"

"No. She works with my dad at his printing business. They drive in together so I can take her car to school. They don't usually get home till six or so."

"Perfect. Let's go."

Luckily, Mrs. Lee's living room window was open. But unless she talked to herself, we weren't going to get anything useful. We set everything up from the back seat of the car and waited.

"This is boring," Suzie said, yawning.

"This is a stakeout. This is what we do; we wait. Have patience. Something will happen."

"How can you be so sure?"

"Because it has to. Have faith, Suz. We're so close."

"Ugh! Don't call me Suz. Just 'cuz you shortened your name doesn't mean you can shorten mine."

"Fair enough, Suzanne." I winked at her.

She rolled her eyes and sighed. "Just call me Suzie, okay? No variations, no nicknames, just plain ol' Suzie. End of discussion." Suzie took a deep, calming breath and picked up the recorder. "What's this recorder for? Why can't we just record it from our phones?"

"The recorder will pick it up through the headphones better. Plus, I'm not turning my phone over to the cops as evidence. If we do get something, we'll have to give the recorder to the police."

"And why did you get a bug? Are you planning to break into her house to put a bug in there? V, you really are crazy."

"I'm not planning to, but I will if I have to. If we don't get anything today, the bug is Plan B."

Five minutes later.

"Oh my gosh, how long do we have to stay slumped down like this? My neck is killing me." Suzie rubbed the back of her neck and groaned.

"The key is to relax. Take deep breaths. Think about your happy place," I said.

"My happy place?"

"You know, a place inside your mind where you can go to relax and unwind. It's where I go when I meditate. My happy place is on a deserted beach on one of the small islands of Hawaii."

"You meditate?"

"Yeah. I mean, it's not really meditation. It's more like—" I paused. "Shh! Someone's coming."

"I'm not the one who was talk—"

"Quiet!" I put my hand up and strained to listen on the headphones.

A maroon minivan pulled into Mrs. Lee's driveway. An Asian man with a scruffy beard got out and walked up to the front porch. Suzie slugged my arm. "That's him! That's the grandson!" she whispered.

"Ouch, you didn't have to hit me so hard. I can see him, ya know. Can you see the license plate?"

Suzie sat up a little higher and peered out through the front windshield. "No, not from here. I'd have to get out of the car to see the back of the van. Should I do that?"

"No, it's too risky. Let's look for it when he leaves. When he backs out we should have a clear view. Now, be quiet so I can listen. Give me the recorder and I'll hold it up to my headphones. Make sure you turn it on first."

Mrs. Lee threw open the screen door in a rage. The guy lunged out of the way to avoid getting hit with it. "You stupid idiot! What are you doing here? I told you to stay away until this whole thing blows over. Don't you know the cops are looking for you?"

"Nah, G, it's all good. They're looking for a blue van. I painted it—see?"

She looked over his shoulder at the badly painted maroon van. She squinted her eyes and hit him over the head. "You worthless moron! Do I have to do everything myself? Get in here, before someone sees you."

They went inside, and she slammed the door.

"Suzie!" I whispered, barely containing my excitement. "She doesn't have a Korean accent!"

"What do you mean? I've never heard her speak before, other than an occasional hi or hello, which now that I think about it was—"

"Never mind that. Listen, when I talked to her two weeks ago, she had a thick Korean accent. She made it seem like she barely knew any English at all. Just now, she spoke to her grandson in 100 percent American English—not even a trace of an accent."

Suzie gulped.

"And did you see how she treated him? Helpless little ol' lady my butt! She's mean! Wow, I bet she's been playing everybody with that act."

"Yeah . . ."

"Wait. She's talking again." I put the headphones back on.

"Why didn't you cut your hair and shave that worthless peach fuzz off like I told you to? They've got a police sketch from the witness at the mall. They show it on the news all the time and it looks just like you. Like I told you, they're looking for *you*, not just a blue van. Painting the stupid van doesn't do anything. You need to get rid of it. Do you even have a brain in there, boy?

"Ever since you took the wrong girl, I've been cleaning up your mess. You are a worthless sack of bones. You're no better than that stupid father of yours, that pathetic excuse of a human being who never visits me."

"But, G, how was I supposed to know *another* girl who looked like the picture you gave me would walk down the same street that morning? It was an honest mistake.

"Besides, I fixed it. I got the right girl at the mall. It was easy, too. All I had to do was get her number. I sent her a text from a 'concerned friend' that I knew her secret and that I was gonna blast it all over the school unless she met me in the mall's parking lot ASAP. She ran right out. Man, you should have seen the look on her face. It was like stealing candy from a baby."

"You did what? You sent her a text? Now your phone number is in her phone, you stupid fool! Where's her phone now?"

"It's all right. I threw it in the Santa Ana River. You gotta relax a little."

"Don't tell me to relax!" I heard a loud whack.

"Ow!"

"What was that? What's happening?" Suzie whispered.

"It sounds like she hit him on the head," I whispered back. "Now shhh. We better be getting all of this. It's a full confession! He's our perp!"

"Our what?"

"Never mind. Shut up and let me listen." I pressed the head-phones against my ears tightly.

"We've been over this a hundred times. The first girl you took is two years younger than the one you were supposed to take. She's too young. Useless. We can't use her. Now we have to figure out how to get rid of her."

Pure joy seized my heart as I realized what Mrs. Lee's words meant. "She's alive. Emma's still alive! I knew it!" I couldn't contain my excitement.

"V be quiet. They'll hear you!" Suzie sounded panicked.

"What was that?" Mrs. Lee looked out the window. "I heard a girl shouting. Did you hear that?"

We flattened ourselves in the back seat and on the floor of Suzie's mom's car, hearts racing.

"I didn't hear anyone, G."

"Oh, what am I asking you for, you stupid boy? Enough of this. You need to leave now and let me think. I have to figure out how to clean up your mess."

"Okay, but—"

"Later! Just go. Now."

"Sorry. Bye, G."

We heard the front door open and close. A couple minutes later, the minivan started up.

Suzie and I didn't move, both too afraid to peer out and try to see the license plate without being seen. I held my breath and squeezed my eyes shut tight, wondering what I'd gotten us into.

We heard the minivan drive away, but we continued to wait until we were sure Mrs. Lee wasn't near her front window. After what seemed like forever, we slowly opened the back door on the driver's side and crawled out, then slunk across the street, staying low to the ground, until we got back to Suzie's house.

AFTER WE'D CRAWLED out of the car and made it back to Suzie's house, we ran up to her room and looked out the window. Mrs. Lee hadn't seen us; we were in the clear.

I jumped up and down on Suzie's bed, elated with our good fortune. "Let's go straight to the police station right now and give Detective Lomeli the recorder. You can drive us there, right? He'll hear Mrs. Lee and her grandson's confession, go arrest them, and make them tell him where Emma and Brylee are. By this time tomorrow, Emma and Brylee will be home where they belong, and we'll be heroes!"

Suzie just stood there, a look of horror on her face.

"Suzie? What's wrong? Suzie? Talk to me," I demanded.

Suzie placed the recorder on the bed in front of me without saying a word. She looked at her feet and shook her head. I looked from the recorder to Suzie and back to the recorder again. Time stopped. Everything from that point on happened in slow motion.

I picked up the recorder and hit play. Nothing happened. I hit rewind. Nothing happened. I hit play again, then fast-forward, then record. The buttons depressed, but the machine's mechanics didn't work. No sound, no voice recording, no *nothing*.

Suzie sank down on the bed next to me. "It's not broken," she said.

"What do you mean it's not broken? Of course it's broken!" I insisted.

"There's no batteries in it. It needs two AA batteries to work. I thought you said you'd tested it?"

"What? No!" I turned the recorder over and opened the

battery compartment. Empty. "I thought it came with batteries!" I wailed.

I buried my face in my hands, "Oh my God, this is all my fault! Now we can't go to the police. We have no proof. Emma is out there somewhere, and Mrs. Lee knows where, and I don't know how to make her tell me. We were so close to getting her back."

Suzie patted my back to comfort me. It didn't work. I was inconsolable. At least she wasn't yelling at me for not putting batteries in the stupid recorder. I was mad enough at myself for the both of us.

"What do we do now?" Suzie asked.

"I have to go home. My mom is going to be back from her treatment soon, and I'm grounded. I have to get back before she gets there. I'll have to think about this and I'll let you know when to start Plan B."

"Plan B?"

"The bug, remember?"

"You're going to put a bug in Mrs. Lee's house? How are you going to do that?"

"I told you, I have to think about it and I'll let you know. I've gotta go. Thanks for helping me on our stakeout today. At least we know who kidnapped Emma and Brylee."

18

GRACE UNDER PRESSURE

Mom greeted me from the living room the second I opened the front door. "V? Could you come in here, please?"

I walked in to find her sitting in an easy chair with a blanket draped over her lap. She looked tired. I averted my eyes and tried to smile. "Hey, Mom. How did it go?"

She sighed. "Round two is done. I haven't had any adverse reactions so far, which is good. I'll get a follow-up PET/CT scan next week to see if the treatments are working. If the tumor is shrinking, I'll continue with three more rounds of chemo, and then surgery."

"That's good news, right?"

"We'll see when the PET scan comes back." Mom looked up at me as if seeing me for the first time. "Where were you just now?"

"I was studying at Suzie's house. I cleared it with you yesterday, and you said I could go," I lied. "Don't you remember?"

Mom shook her head, "Nope, I have no memory of that

conversation. Damn chemo brain. Oh! Speaking of conversations! Guess who I got a call from today?"

"Um ... the President?"

"Very funny, miss smarty-pants. No, not the President." Mom paused dramatically and continued, "The Orange Fire Department called and asked me to be their 'Pinktober Girl.' They raise money throughout the month of October every year to donate to various cancer foundations for Breast Cancer Awareness Month. They choose a local person to sponsor each year, and this year they chose me. They'll have restaurant-sponsored events downtown, sell T-shirts, and more, all to raise money and awareness. And October 1st, they're coming to our school to honor me. It's kind of surreal, don't you think?"

"Wow. Yeah, like you're the poster girl for breast cancer?"

"Well, it doesn't sound as cool when you put it that way, but something like that. It will give me a chance to raise money and make a difference. Everyone has already helped me so much. I want to be able to give back somehow. This is a good platform for that."

"Yeah, Mom. That sounds good. But what's 'chemo brain'? Is the cancer in your brain now?"

"Oh no, honey! It's nothing like that, nothing to worry about. I just call it that. What I meant was, all the stuff they pump through me each chemotherapy session takes a toll on my body and it messes with my short-term memory. It makes me feel foggy-headed, among other things." She stopped talking, as if considering how much or what to tell me.

Hmm, this little piece of info could come in quite handy. Perhaps I can use this 'foggy brain' side effect to my advantage from time to time. I'll definitely remember this!

"Sweetie, you know I like to stay positive as much as I can," Mom continued softly. "But I gotta be honest with you. Chemo sucks! I'm definitely feeling this one more than the last one. And I think they're going to get harder as I go. But I hear that having bad side effects means that the chemo is working.

"The side effects are rotten, though. Tomorrow, the chemo treatment will kick in after the steroids wear off. It feels like a hangover of sorts, I hear."

"A hangover? Do you mean like getting sick after drinking too much alcohol?"

"Well, yes. Sorry, sometimes I forget I'm talking to a 14-year-old." Mom took a deep breath. "I anticipate I'll spend most of tomorrow with my head in the toilet, which has been compared to drinking too much and being hungover the next day. You have so much to learn, young grasshopper."

"It's not funny, Mom. That's terrible! I don't want you to be puking all day. That sounds awful. I hate what this is doing to you."

"It's okay, sweetheart," my mother's melodic voice soothed. "Come here, let me look at you."

I knelt down next to her chair. She took my hand in hers and gazed into my eyes, straight through to my soul, the way only my mom had ever looked at me. She steeled herself and with a strong, confident voice said, "I can take it. You know me. I'm a fighter—'grace under pressure.' You know who said that, right?"

"Ernest Hemingway?"

"That's my girl. Your middle name's not Hemingway for nothing." She dropped my hand and winked.

I rolled my eyes.

"During an interview with Dorothy Parker, Hemingway's definition of guts, or courage, was 'grace under pressure.' I've always loved that definition, and now I will strive to live up to it."

I shook my head and laughed, saying, "Only you would know something like that."

"Not true. Hemingway has a huge fan club." Mom laughed, too. "The right attitude is everything," she added with fervor. "Besides, it's better than the alternative."

"The alternative?"

"Being dead."

"Mom!"

"Don't you worry, baby girl. I'm not going anywhere. Not for a long time. But in the meantime, I have to keep putting this toxic shit into my body to get out the worse toxic shit—the cancer. It will buy me more time, and it will be worth it.

"But right now, this toxic shit is messing with my taste buds; even water tastes awful. Dad is at Sprouts finding me healthy snacks that will magically infiltrate my taste buds. Oh! That reminds me, there's a freshly made chicken casserole in the kitchen. Lisa just dropped it off."

Happy for the subject change, I jumped up to my feet and ventured toward the kitchen. "I wondered what that delicious-smelling aroma was. Where does she keep finding all these people for this meal train? We've never eaten so good. I hope it never stops."

"Hey, you don't like my cooking?"

"Since when do you even cook?" I teased.

"V, stop giving your mother a hard time," Dad called out from the front door as he came in with Scotty. "If you want to help out, why don't you set the table and start dishing up that amazing-smelling casserole that your sweet, loving mother didn't cook?" He winked at me as he came in and kissed Mom on the forehead.

I'd heard more than enough about cancer and chemo lately, more than I'd ever wanted to, and relief swept over me as I left

the room to set the table. It was something mindless to do—
busy work. And right now, I didn't want to think about
anything.

It had been an emotionally draining day . . . from learning
that Mrs. Lee and her grandson were the ones who kidnapped
Emma, yet I was no closer to finding her, to my mom suffering
more than she'd been letting on—it was too much. My brain
and my heart needed a break. I'd had about all I could handle.

WHEN I FINISHED WASHING the dinner dishes and cleaning up
the kitchen, I excused myself and went up to my room. I
collapsed on the bed and replayed Suzie's shocking discovery
over and over in my mind.

*How could I be so stupid? I thought I'd been so well prepared. I'll
never forgive myself for my careless mistake.*

19
PHONE CALL

A week went by without any news. Suzie kept watch on Mrs. Lee's house as much as she could. The grandson hadn't returned, and Mrs. Lee never had any other visitors. Her house was dark and quiet. As far as Suzie could tell, she never went anywhere, so how was I supposed to get in there to plant a bug? She even had her groceries delivered.

I tried to go to the police station to talk to Lomeli, but my dad intercepted and grounded me again. He told me to leave the police alone and let them do their job. I couldn't even tell him Emma was alive because I'd lied and snuck out of the house to find out, not to mention I'd put Suzie and myself at risk by listening to Mrs. Lee's conversation with her grandson.

Besides, Suzie was right. Who was going to believe us? Suzie was a geeky outcast who barely talked to anyone. She spent most of her free time at school in the Chem Lab or with her nose in a book. And I was already labeled the strange freak who daydreams about being a great teen detective, living in a fantasy world and not in touch with reality. *Everyone thinks I'm delusional as it is, why give them more ammunition?*

Nope. I couldn't tell anyone what I knew. And I couldn't rely on anyone else to find Emma either, especially since Lomeli pretty much told me they think Emma is dead and they have no leads. I needed to step up my game. I needed to find Emma myself.

I SAT at the dinner table with my family, but I wasn't really there. I was lost in thought, trying to come up with a way to track Mrs. Lee's grandson because it became painfully clear to me that Mrs. Lee would never lead me to Emma. I felt like I'd reached a dead end. To get this far, to know she's alive, and not be able to track her—it was maddening!

If only I could find out where this guy lives. He's the one who kidnapped her; he must have her hidden somewhere. He has to! Think! Hmm, Mrs. Lee mentioned a son who doesn't visit her. I wonder if I could find him.

I pictured myself at the moment I found Mrs. Lee's son, Sam Lee.

I knocked on the door to his house. No one answered. I turned the knob, but the door was locked. I went around the back and found the glass slider unlocked. I eased it open and tiptoed inside the dark house.

I heard a noise downstairs. Downstairs? I thought to myself. Since when do houses in Orange, California, have basements?

I held my breath as I crept silently down the hidden stairwell. At the bottom of the stairs was a door. I reached out and tested the knob. Thankfully, it was unlocked. I pushed open the door as my heart raced, excitement and adrenaline rushing through me.

"V? Brylee, wake up! V's here! She found us! Oh, V! I knew you

would find me!" Emma shouted at me through the bars of her cage in a corner of the dark basement. She reached her arm out through the bars and waved at me.

Brylee rubbed her eyes and sat up. "What's going on?"

"V's here! She's come to rescue us!" Emma squealed.

I could barely contain my excitement as I ran over to the cage to open it. "Emma! Are you okay? Brylee, are you okay?" I rattled the cage door. "This cage is locked. How do I get you out of here?"

"There's a key over there." Emma pointed across the room. "They keep it in plain sight on that table just to toy with us."

I ran over to the table and found the key. I opened the cage door to let Emma and Brylee out when suddenly Emma's face froze in fear as we heard a noise on the stairs. "V? V! V, where are you?"

"V? V! V, where are you right now?" Mom shouted at me.

"Huh? What?" I shook my head to clear my mind. "Oh, Mom. Sorry. What were you saying?"

"Where were you just now? You seemed so far away. Is everything all right?"

"Of course, Mom. I'm fine. Why are you worrying about me? You're the one who had a PET scan today. How did it go? When do you get your results from the scans?"

"Nice try. You were a million miles away just now and I'm not supposed to be concerned? V, it's a mother's job to be concerned. And yes, my PET scan was today; I'm surprised you remembered."

"Mom. Give me some credit, geesh." I folded my arms across my chest and sighed. "Of course I remembered—so when will you get the results?"

"Thursday."

"But that's October 1st." I frowned.

"So?"

"So, aren't you 'Pinktober Girl' or something?"

"You don't miss a thing, do you?"

"Nope. So, how are you going to do both? Mom, you have to be there—you're their star attraction."

"It's simple. The appointment to get my test results isn't until after school. I'll be there for the festivities, don't worry."

"I'm counting on it," I teased.

MY PHONE RANG JUST as I finished loading the dishwasher with dinner dishes. I ran to grab it, as it was still sitting on the kitchen table, and then nearly dropped it when I saw the caller's name. I stared at it.

ROSA MORENO. Emma's mom. Hope and dread competed for center stage in my thoughts while I fought down the rising panic in my throat.

"Hello?" I tried to sound hopeful, upbeat.

"V! I'm so glad I got a hold of you." Rosa said, sobbing into her phone such that I had to pull mine away from my ear. *She's glad? But it sounds like she's crying.* "They found her! They found my Emma!"

My heart thudded in my ears. I didn't know if this was good news or bad. I didn't know what to ask, how to react. I raced up the stairs and into my room, slamming the door shut behind me so I could talk to Emma's mom in private and uninterrupted. If my parents overheard my conversation, they'd want to talk to her, too. This call was just for *me*.

"V? Are you still there?"

"Yes, I'm still here," I said breathlessly. "I just ran up to my room for some privacy." I paused. "Um . . . is she . . . is she alive?"

"Oh! Yes! I'm so happy that I'm crying tears of joy, but you probably thought I was crying because—Oh, V, I'm so sorry. Emma's alive! Mija is alive! I'm so happy!"

"I knew it! I just knew it!" Tears sprang to my eyes as I took in the good news. "That's awesome! Where is she? Can I see her? Is she okay?"

"Well, they don't have her yet."

"Wait—what? Who doesn't have her? Where is she?"

"She's in Portland, Oregon."

"What do you mean? I don't understand. Why is she in Portland?"

"They don't know. Someone in Portland saw her picture on the news. They called the police to report they saw her in downtown Portland this morning."

"Are you sure? But how can that be?"

"Yes, yes. They're sure. They didn't want to call me until they knew for sure. I just got off the phone with Detective Lomeli. He's working with the Child Exploitation Task Force in the Portland FBI. He said they received other tips on their hotline matching Emma's description. They think the kidnappers still have her, and they're monitoring the situation very closely."

"I knew she was alive. This whole time, I never doubted it."

"I know, V. Me, too. You've been such a good friend to my Emma. I know you kept looking for her, even when the police stopped. Thank you, V. You kept hope alive for me."

"How could the kidnappers still have her? Did they drive her up to Portland? Why? Maybe she got away and is trying to get back to us! Is Lomeli up there now? Did he go to Portland to find her and bring her back?"

"V, slow down. I'm sorry, I don't know. No, Lomeli's not going up there. He said it's out of his jurisdiction. He said that the FBI will handle it now."

"But why?"

"He said that because the kidnappers crossed state lines with a minor it has now become a federal case. It's under the FBI's jurisdiction."

"No! That's not right. Someone needs to be up there looking for her."

"But the FBI are—"

"What else did Lomeli tell you? Is there anything else that you can tell me? Any other leads or clues?"

"Only that Emma was seen with some other girls this morning at Pioneer Square. That's all he would tell me."

"Pioneer Square?"

"Yes, that's what he said."

"Okay, thanks. I can work with that."

"V? What do you mean you 'can work with that'? You're not going up there, are you?"

"Don't worry, Rosa. It will all be okay. Like you said, the FBI will find her and bring her home. Hey, in a few days, she'll be home with us where she belongs!"

"I hope so, V. I hope so. I miss my little girl so much. I can't believe it's been nearly a month since I last saw my baby."

"I know. Me too. Just have faith, Rosa. Emma will be back home with us soon—I just know it."

I clicked the button to end the call, set my phone down on my nightstand, and jumped into action. Which, at the moment, meant pacing around my room so I could come up with a plan to get myself to Portland without my parents reporting *me* missing. *Think, V. Think!*

20
PINKTOBER

Two days later on October 1st, Mom, Dad, and I showed up at school to see people dressed in pink everywhere. It was day one of Breast Cancer Awareness Month, and Sierra High School went all out in support of one of their own.

The walls were littered with posters. Twitter and Instagram hashtags abounded: #findthecure, #endthefight, #cancersucks, #pinktober, #fcancer, et cetera. It went on and on. Staff and students alike had on pink shirts, pants, shorts, skirts, sweatshirts, jackets, hoodies, tights, socks, shoes, fingernails, wristbands, jewelry, pins—even pink hair. It looked like someone had projectile vomited Pepto Bismol all over my school. I was horrified.

But not Mom. She loved every minute of it. After all, it was all in her honor. She'd been unofficially voted 'favorite teacher' by her students every year since she'd been there, and she'd officially won the Teacher of the Year Award numerous times. Everyone loved her.

Don't get me wrong. I loved her, too—duh. Of course I

loved her. She was my mom. But being in her shadow? Not so much fun. Also, now I had to be surrounded by pink for a month. *Please, Lord, just take me now.* Okay, not funny. But—I *hate* pink.

JUST BEFORE THE end of second period, Dr. Fitz's voice boomed over the intercom announcing a special surprise appearance by the Orange Fire Department and their pink fire engine. "So come on out to the quad to help the fire department honor and support our very own Mrs. J," he finished. Our school had a fifteen-minute break between second and third periods every day. Dr. Fitz encouraged us to socialize and participate in various break-time activities throughout the year. He said it was good for student morale and school spirit.

"Hey, V, isn't that your mom?" Jacob sneered.

"Yeah, so?" I shot back.

"So, what's the fire department gonna do? Hose her down? Ha ha ha!"

"Jacob. That's quite enough, young man." Miss McCully, our AP Biology teacher, glared at Jacob.

By the look on her face, he decided to leave me alone. Luckily, the bell rang, and I got out of there as fast as I could.

I walked out to the quad and looked for a place to blend in. *Okay, who am I kidding?* I looked for a place to hide. I knew Mom was about to be the center of attention, and I didn't want any attention drawn to me because of it. I found a clump of upperclassmen to stand behind. They had no idea who I was, and that was just fine with me.

Hundreds of pink-clad students and staff gathered around

in anticipation of seeing a pink fire truck for the first time. Seconds later, we heard the familiar blast of a fire engine's air horn as we spotted the pink truck, a "rolling tribute for those affected by breast cancer," drive through the center of our campus and pull right up to the steps of the quad.

Every year, the Orange Fire Department wraps their fire engine in bright pink material, patterned with darker pink cancer ribbons all over it, and the firefighters wear pink shirts. They sponsor a different person each year. This year their 'poster girl' was none other than my mom, Hannah Jiménez.

Dr. Fitz stood at the top of the stairs, microphone in hand, waiting for the firefighters to join him. Of course, he was wearing a powder pink button-up dress shirt, with a dark pink tie and gray slacks, for the occasion.

He called Mr. and Mrs. J up to the stage, made a few brief announcements and introductions, then handed the microphone to the fire captain, Steve Weller.

A firefighting crew of about ten men and two women stood in two neat rows behind their chief. They wore pink T-shirts emblazoned with "Orange FIRE" and their navy uniform pants. They stood proud as the chief presented my mother with a certificate and their pledge to raise money and awareness for the cancer charity of her choosing.

Dr. Fitz took the microphone back and finally introduced Mrs. Hannah Jiménez, the moment we were all waiting for. Suddenly, all eyes were on my mom and the quad was silent as she took the mic.

My dad stood by her side, sporting a pale pink T-shirt emblazoned with "Team Hannah" and a breast cancer ribbon. Naturally, one of his students had the shirt made for him.

Then there was my mom. She wore a plain, loose-fitting pink T-shirt and long tan skirt, with her cute red wig in pigtails, and a bandana over the wig. This was her moment—and she delivered.

"I found out I had stage four breast cancer the day before my 39th birthday, about a month ago. Since that time, not a single act of kindness has gone unnoticed by our family. Every prayer, gesture, word, email, text, post, call, card, poem, meal, pink T-shirt, pink wristband . . ."

The crowd laughed.

Mom continued, ". . . promise, thought, hope, smile, note, and flower has helped us through every moment. They have made us stronger. Thank you.

"To be part of such a big cause, and to help draw attention to such an important cause as well, I . . . I don't know how to describe the level of support I've felt from this school, from this staff, from my family. Um, from all the administration—at our school and at the district . . . and I just want you to know that I'm going to beat this. And I'm going to beat this because . . ."

The crowd cheered so loud they drowned her out. Mom put her hand out to quiet them, and then waited patiently for the crowd to settle. *Just like a teacher*, I couldn't help but think as I watched her command the crowd into silence again, with only her body language and stoic expression.

". . . and all of the love and support that you have shown us. You have made all the difference in our lives and through this fight, and we love you. Ernest Hemingway said that people are 'strong in the broken places.' I plan on not just living but living up to that statement. Thank you."

Mom gave the microphone to the fire captain while the crowd roared with thunderous applause. She fell into Dad's outstretched arms, overcome with emotion.

The KABC news crew was even there to capture the event,

and Mom made the five o'clock news. It was surreal. Their motto this year was to "extinguish cancer."

A reporter interviewed my mom, then the fire chief asked her to take a spin in their fire engine. She climbed in, cheeks flushed, and grinning from ear to ear. The fire engine took a lap around the quad, and she happily waved out the window like she was the princess of the parade.

The truck stopped at the steps and let her out. She was given a black Sharpie pen and the honor of being the first one to sign the pink-clad fire truck. She signed her name big, right in the front, between the headlights. A bunch of people took pictures, then the firefighters passed out Sharpies and said anyone who had been affected by cancer in some personal way could sign the pink-clad fire truck. Before long, it was covered in heartfelt messages, hearts, and signatures.

AFTER SCHOOL, I raced home to pack while Mom and Dad went to her doctor's appointment to get her test results. The day had been emotional, and I wanted to put it behind me as fast as I could. This was no time to worry about my mom. It was time to find Emma, and I had a flight booked to Portland early the next morning.

21

GOING TO PORTLAND

Five minutes after I'd gotten the call from Rosa that Emma had been spotted in Portland, I had thought of a plan. I typed a letter 'from Aunt Karen' on an old IBM Selectric typewriter that my mom kept for who knows why, but I was thankful I had access to it because Aunt Karen was old school. She didn't even own a computer or mobile phone, so no emailing and texting. She always typed her letters to us, which would make this letter easy to forge.

While posing as Aunt Karen, I (I mean she) asked me to come up and spend the weekend with her. I made up a story about Kristen Bell coming to Portland for a one-weekend-only special charity event, and my aunt had won two tickets from a local radio station giveaway. Everyone knew what a huge Kristen Bell fan I was, so I knew that it would be tough for my parents to say no.

Letter finished, signature forged, I made a big deal out of checking the mail, even though it was eight o'clock at night. Since I was the one who brought in the mail 98 percent of the time, no one questioned this.

I walked out to the mailbox and opened it. It was empty. I slipped Aunt Karen's letter inside, took a deep breath, and squared my shoulders. "It's showtime," I whispered to myself.

I grabbed the letter out and ripped off the envelope, wadding it up in my hand (no canceled postage stamp). I stayed outside long enough to "read" the letter. Then I ran up to the house, threw open the front door, and delivered the academy award-winning performance of a lifetime.

"Mom! Dad!" I ran into the living room breathless and shouting, "Aunt Karen just invited me to Portland for the weekend! She has tickets to a special engagement interview with Kristen Bell! Can I go? Can I go? Please? All my homework's done, and I'll clean the house for two weeks without complaining. What do you say, huh? Pretty please?"

Mom and Dad exchanged a look. "May I see the letter?" Mom held out her hand.

I gave her the letter and held my breath while she read it, hoping it sounded like something my crazy great aunt would write.

"Huh. How 'bout that." Mom shook her head.

"What's your nutty Aunt Karen up to now?" Dad asked.

"It says she won the tickets from a radio contest she entered because she knows how much V loves Kristen Bell. It says she misses her great niece and wants to spend time with her. What do you think we should do, Carlos?"

"Don't look at me," Dad said and threw his hands up. "She's your aunt."

I gave Mom the Bambi eyes and stared her down.

She sighed and said, "Okay, you can go."

"Really? Yay! Thank you, Mom! Thank you so much!" I flung my arms around her.

"Easy there, tiger." Mom laughed and winced at the same time.

"Sorry." I backed off. "Did that hurt? I didn't mean to hurt you."

"You didn't. It was just a little tight, that's all. I'll book your flight right now. With such short notice, I can't imagine it'll be cheap, and Aunt Karen doesn't have much money these days. I'm just glad she won the tickets and doesn't have to pay an arm and a leg for this sudden surprise visit."

Mom didn't even call Aunt Karen to confirm. I couldn't believe how easy it had been to fool them. She also gave me money because Aunt Karen was retired and lived alone. Mom didn't want her to have to spend extra money on me.

And I especially love how my mom insisted on paying for my flight. She called Alaska Airlines herself and booked a roundtrip ticket for an unaccompanied minor to Portland, leaving Friday morning and returning Monday afternoon. I would even get to miss two days of school. This plan could not have worked out better. I couldn't believe my luck, and I was beyond excited.

AT LAST, Friday arrived. I was packed and ready to go when Grandma showed up at 5:55 a.m. to drive me to the airport. It had been easy to get up early since I'd been awake most of the night anyway.

This is actually happening! I'm going to Portland to find Emma!

The adrenaline coursed through my veins as I rushed through the house, careful not to make too much noise and wake anyone else up.

Mom said she had a doctor's appointment later that morning. Dad wanted to go with her, so they'd asked Grandma to take me to the airport. I didn't care who took me, as long as I made that flight. I was going to rescue Emma.

I can just see the look on Lomeli's smug face when he realizes a kid has solved this case single-handedly. I'll be a hero. And, most importantly, I'll have Emma back.

"Violet! Snap out of it. Hello? Have you heard a word I've said?" I could hear the frustrated tone in Grandma's voice. I blinked a couple times to clear my head and watched her merge onto the freeway.

"Sorry, Grandma. I was just thinking about my trip. I'm so excited!"

"I see. You seemed a thousand miles away just now. I guess you're already there." She laughed at her own joke. "I asked you if you've been keeping in touch with my sister, your great-aunt Karen?"

"Oh. No, not really."

"Well, I'm certainly surprised she arranged this weekend trip. This is very uncharacteristic of her. She's been such a recluse lately. She rarely answers her phone when I call her. You tell her to call her sister once in a while, will you?"

"Of course, Grandma. I'm sure she just got busy with one of her projects." The truth was I had no idea what Aunt Karen was up to these days. I hadn't seen her in three years, since the last time she visited us, and I'd never been to visit her.

I'd never even been to Portland before. The only time I'd ever been to Oregon was last winter, when my family took a ski trip to Central Oregon over Christmas break. We got snowed in, and I got to go skiing for the first time. And my mom told the mesmerizing story about the glass stars for the first time, the one Scotty insists on hearing over and over. I loved that trip.

But Aunt Karen? Dad was right. Aunt Karen could definitely be described as a bit 'nutty.' She lived alone, except for a few cats. Even though she'd worked at an adoption agency for over forty years, she'd never had any children of her own, adopted or naturally. She never married, and as far as I knew, had never even been in love or had a relationship.

She'd retired shortly after we adopted Scotty, six years ago. She used to visit us every year and stay a couple weeks, saying she needed a break from the rain. But it had been three years since her last visit.

The thing about Aunt Karen was she told really long stories, the same stories, over and over. She could talk endlessly. Funny, probably the real reason my mom had agreed so readily to this trip was because she didn't want to call Aunt Karen and spend an hour and a half on the phone with her. I didn't even think Aunt Karen knew about Mom's cancer. We kind of stopped keeping in touch with her, but I was surprised to hear she didn't take Grandma's calls.

I don't know what's going on there, but if I'm lucky, I won't find out this trip. And Aunt Karen won't even know I was ever in town.

"Are you sure you don't want me to come in with you?" Grandma burst in on my thoughts again, waking me from my reverie.

"Grandma, I told you. I have a special boarding pass that says, 'Unaccompanied Minor.' That means an airline employee will escort me to my gate and make sure I get on the plane. I'll be fine. Besides, they won't let you go to the gate with me anyway since you don't have a boarding pass."

"All right, if you're sure. My, Violet, you're growing up so fast."

Grandma pulled the car up to the curb of the departures

area at John Wayne Airport. We both got out of the car, and I grabbed my backpack.

"Is that the only luggage you have?"

"It's all I need. I travel light."

I hugged Grandma, and she whispered in my ear, "Don't let my sister drive you crazy. Have a safe flight, dear."

"I will. Thanks, Grandma. Bye."

"Bye, V. Have fun."

Sitting in my seat, 7B, which was the middle seat of three on the Boeing 737, I couldn't believe how smooth it had all gone so far. I had an escort from the moment I handed over my boarding pass at the airline check-in counter—and I got to pre-board.

This traveling alone thing is easy. What did I ever have to be nervous about?

Just then, an older woman, I'd say she was around 70, dropped her purse and jacket down on the aisle seat next to me. Without saying a word, she abruptly crossed in front of me and sat down in the window seat. I took my sweatshirt off the aisle seat next to me and apologized, assuming it was her assigned seat. She didn't budge. She didn't even act like she heard me. She just turned and stared out the window, leaving her stuff on the aisle seat.

Confused, I was about to say something when an elderly man, about the same age, stopped at the aisle seat, 7C, next to me. He bent down and took the purse and jacket off the seat then he reached over me and handed them to the woman. He sat down next to me without saying a word.

I smiled at him and said, "This is my first time flying by myself. It's also my first time going to Portland."

The man grunted toward me.

The woman took a neck pillow out of her purse, blew it up, and placed it around her neck.

The man snickered and said, "Where'd ya get that?"

"Oh, I don't remember." She sighed. "I've had it."

"Do you two know each other?" I asked, looking back and forth from one to the other.

"He's my husband," the woman answered.

"Oh! Do you want to sit by him? I can move," I offered.

"Nope," she replied, tight-lipped. She stared straight ahead without an ounce of mirth or humor in her expression.

Neither one of them said another word for the duration of the two-and-a-half-hour flight. They read or closed their eyes, and the man elbowed me repeatedly; I tucked both my arms in and gave up the armrests.

They seemed sad. Miserable. I wondered what their story was. I figured they were either unhappily married, or on their way to a funeral. *Or maybe both.* I shuddered.

Why don't they love each other like my parents do? Dad still does sweet things for Mom all the time. And her face lights up every time. I can't imagine them ever treating each other so cold and dismissive —like this couple. How sad it must be not to love the person you're married to.

I wanted to scream at them, *My mom has cancer, you idiots! Stop being so mean to each other! Stop taking each other for granted!* And then it hit me. The way I'd lied to my parents to get on this flight. That I'd been avoiding my mom and sneaking around. That I'd been less than kind. That I had taken her for granted.

Nope. I'm not going there right now. I've got to find Emma!

Thankfully, it had been easy to figure out how to get from the airport to downtown Portland. I boarded a MAX light rail at the airport and transferred to a TriMet bus that would take me downtown. Public transit here seemed to be a breeze—and no one cared that a kid was traveling alone. I stared at a woman sitting across from me on the bus as I tried to come up with a plan. She wore a long purple skirt, and beautiful silver-gray hair flowed around her face and down to her waist. On her left wrist was a mass of colorful bracelets; some were made of yarn, some beads, and others, a rubbery plastic. One bracelet in particular caught my eye. It was bright blue and made out of rubber. I let myself zone out on it as I once again got lost in my thoughts.

What am I going to do when I get downtown? I really didn't think this through very well. My only lead is that Emma has been seen downtown somewhere. I don't even know where to start looking.

I sighed out loud, still staring at the bracelet and wondering what to do next. The bracelet had the letters "WWJD" stamped in big white letters on it. The woman wearing it looked up at me and smiled.

"I see you've noticed my bracelet," she said.

"Um, yeah," I replied and looked down sheepishly.

"Do you know what WWJD stands for?"

"Uh, no," I admitted.

"It stands for 'What would Jesus do?' It's a reminder to me to live my life the same way Jesus would, as much as I can. When I'm faced with big decisions, I ask myself, 'What would Jesus do if he were in my place?' It helps me to focus, and to hopefully make the right decision."

I smiled at her and thought about what she said. "Thanks for telling me that. I think it's a great way to try to live your life."

"Do you believe in Jesus?"

"Well, my family isn't very religious, but we've been to church a few times. I'm not really sure what I believe in yet, but I just think it's a good idea to stop and think, to try to do the right thing when faced with a big decision."

"How very astute of you. My, you are a bright girl, aren't you?"

I squirmed. *Great. She thinks I'm a little kid.* I didn't feel like talking to her anymore. I smiled at her one last time, then turned away to look out the window at the rainy streets.

I kept thinking about that silly bracelet. *WWJD.*

Then it donned on me. *What would Veronica do?* I knew she was just a fictional character on a TV show, but I was desperate. I had to start thinking like a detective—any detective. Real or fiction, what's the difference? At this point, I just needed a plan.

★ ★ ★ ★ ★

THANKFULLY, it had stopped raining by the time I got off the bus near the Portland Visitor Center, which was my intended destination. I walked three short blocks to SW Taylor Street, grateful for the map on my iPhone, and stood in front of the visitor center. Since I had no idea where to start looking, I figured this was my best bet. All I knew from what Rosa had told me was that Emma had been spotted in Pioneer Square, in the downtown area of Southwest Portland.

I took a deep breath, pushed the door open, and walked inside. I walked up to the information counter and asked where Pioneer Square was.

"I think you must mean Pioneer *Courthouse* Square. It's an open courtyard area comprised of 40,000 square feet of over 80,000 personalized inscribed bricks."

"Wow, that's a *ton* of bricks—er, actually, several tons." I laughed at my lame joke. The lady helping me did not. I got out my phone, ready to look it up and asked, "Where can I find this amazing display of masonry?"

"Two blocks down, on 6th Avenue. You can't miss it." She turned away and went back to her uneaten food. I guess I interrupted her lunch.

"Thank you," I replied. I walked out the door and down the street two blocks, and there it was, just like she said—a veritable sea of red bricks in the middle of the city.

"Now what?" I asked to no one. I took in my surroundings and inhaled deeply, taking in the cool air, noticing the fresh and clean scent after the rains. The courtyard was a giant square, with columns on the perimeter and a waterfall fountain. The center of the square looked like an amphitheater with a semicircle of brick steps arranged like stadium seats. Each brick under my feet had someone's name inscribed on it, all the way across the square until I reached the steps.

As I walked over to the steps, I began muttering to myself, "Was Emma really here? How? Why? Will she be back? Who was she with? Why did they take her? How the heck am I going to find her in this city?" My head was spinning with questions, and I didn't have any answers.

I took my backpack off, set it down on the wet steps, and then sat on it. I hadn't prepared for the weather when I'd hastily packed. All I had was my black SHS hooded sweatshirt. It was October 2nd and still warm and sunny where I lived. It hadn't even occurred to me that it would be cold or rainy here.

I sighed and put my head in my hands. Suddenly the dam burst and the torrent of emotions I'd held back for the past month flowed out of me. The anguish of my soul matched the dark storm clouds over my head. I burst into gut-wrenching sobs.

This wasn't soft, quiet crying. No. It was loud, ugly, snot-filled wailing—guttural and primal. My sides heaved in and out, I couldn't catch my breath, and my heart felt like it was being squeezed from inside my chest.

A hand landed softly on my shoulder. I jumped.

"Hey little girl. It's okay. It can't be that bad, can it?" a young Asian girl sat down beside me and put her arm around me. She wore faded overalls and a long blue coat made of fake fur. The sleeves were too short. Her shiny black hair was in pigtails. I guessed she was probably 12.

"You're calling *me* a little girl? Who are you? What are you doing here without your parents? Why aren't you in school?" I stared at her openly while wiping the wetness off my face with my sweatshirt sleeves.

"Hey, girl, I could ask you the same questions." She stared back at me with a brazen look in her eyes that defied her young age. Then a smile slowly crept across her face. "You stopped crying. What an awful sound it was. Waah waaaa waah! Ew!" She made a sour face, and we both laughed.

"Thanks. I never cry like that. It's just that . . . I guess I'm feeling kind of hopeless right now."

"Sure you don't," she said and winked at me. "I'm Mèimei. It means 'younger sister' in Chinese. But my brother calls me 'Méi-méi,' which means 'no-no.' He says I was a mistake, a no-no."

"That's terrible. He sounds like a jerk."

"Yes, well, he can be a real jerk sometimes, but he's mostly okay. I'm not in school today because it is a teacher-in-service day. Auntie doesn't know. She thinks I'm at school. I go to Lincoln, a few blocks from here."

We sat in silence for a moment, watching people in their fancy suits hurry across the square to their important appointments. It was lunchtime in the city.

Mèimei spoke again, "I come here all the time. Great hangout spot. But I've never seen you before. What's your name? Where did you come from?"

"I'm V, and I just got here. I flew in this morning from California, and I'm looking for my friend. You say you come here all the time?"

"Yep."

"Well, maybe you've seen my friend?"

"Is her name Emma?"

"YES! How did you know? Do you know where she is? Is she okay?"

"Hold on there, V. I haven't seen her."

My face fell. "But how do you know her name?"

"You just said it a moment ago, when you were talking to yourself."

"You heard me?"

"Of course I heard you. Mèimei hears everything. I'm very quiet. You didn't hear me sneak up on you, right?"

I shook my head. "You snuck up on me?"

"Yes. Sort of. No, not really. But I walked very quietly." She looked me up and down. "I can help you find your friend but not with you dressed like that."

"You can find her? How? What's wrong with the way I'm dressed? What does that have to do with—"

"Quiet. Girl, you ask a lot of questions. Just stop for a minute. Let me think."

"Okay, sorry." I stared at the sea of bricks across the courtyard and we sat in silence while Mèimei decided how she was going to help me find Emma. If she really could help me like she said she could, I suddenly felt very lucky to have met her. Relief swept over me as I let someone else do the thinking, for a change.

23

THE PLAN

An hour later, Mèimei and I were instant friends. We quickly learned that we both looked much younger than our real ages. She was actually a year *older* than me. When I asked her why she dressed so young, in overalls and pigtails, a darkness crossed her face.

"I'll tell you later," she said.

We came up with a plan, and before I knew it, we had walked four blocks to Goodwill, bought my disguise, and hopped on a bus to Chinatown. I loved how everything in Portland was so easy to get to—and that the city blocks were short. Nothing like the long, confusing blocks in Los Angeles.

Mèimei and her brother, Qiang, lived in a small apartment above the Red Dragon massage parlor. Their aunt, whom Mèimei called 'Auntie,' owned the parlor, and Qiang helped her run it. Mèimei wasn't allowed to go inside unless it was an emergency. She said her ma gave her the same advice over and over. She cleared her throat and suddenly took on a heavy accent, imitating her mother: "You no want this life. You smart girl. You grow up to be brilliant doctor, care for Ma in old age."

We both giggled.

Mèimei was told that her parents had been killed in a tragic car accident two years ago. Auntie and Qiang were all she had left. But they were always too busy running the massage parlor, so Mèimei spent a lot of time alone. She often did her homework at the Multnomah County Library downtown, or at Pioneer Courthouse Square.

She hated staying in the apartment alone. She said that every time she looked out the window she saw creepy-looking men coming and going at all hours. They made her skin crawl. She also said the massage therapists who worked there didn't seem to stay very long, and that her Aunt complained about constantly having to train new girls.

We got off the bus and walked a couple blocks to Mèimei's apartment. She stopped in front of the red door at the massage parlor and put her finger up to her lips. She listened at the door for what seemed like an eternity, then finally motioned me over. We tiptoed upstairs, and I held my breath until we got to her bedroom.

"What was that all about?" I asked, dreading what she might say.

"Auntie can't know about you. It's not safe."

"What do you mean 'it's not safe'? What are you talking about?"

"You promise not to tell?"

"I'm not promising anything!" I exclaimed.

"Shh. V, you must keep your voice down. Please. It's for your safety." Mèimei's eyes widened as she pleaded for me to calm down.

"My *safety*?" I clenched my jaw and balled up my hands into fists. I took a deep breath and tried to calm down. I dropped my voice down low and quiet, speaking slowly. "My best friend was kidnapped a thousand miles from here a month ago. Witnesses —here in Portland—reported seeing a girl who looks like the picture they saw of Emma on the news a few days ago. Then you turn up by my side because you overhear me crying about my missing friend and you tell me you can help me find her. *Mèimei, what do you know?* What aren't you telling me?"

Mèimei flopped down onto her bed. Her shoulders slumped, and she cast her eyes down. She stayed like that for a long time. Finally, she looked up at me with tears in her eyes. "You better sit down. You're not gonna like what I'm about to tell you."

I sat down on a wooden chair by her desk, afraid to speak. I somehow felt that what she was about to tell me was hard for her to say but also very important. I didn't want to say anything that might make her change her mind.

"Auntie treats me like a little girl. She thinks I don't know what goes on around here. I know she's only trying to protect me. Trying to keep me out of the business. She makes me dress like a tomboy. I have to wear baggy clothes. I can't even wear a bra or any makeup. She says I can't ever look sexy. She says sexy is bad. She says sexy causes problems." She stopped talking and looked at me expectantly.

"Mèimei, I'm sorry, but I have no idea what you're talking about. What does this have to do with Emma? Why did we just buy slutty hooker clothes at Goodwill? You're going to have to spell it out for me. I don't understand any of this. I just want my best friend back."

"I think Auntie is a pimp!" she blurted.

"What? Are you crazy? You want me to dress like a prostitute so your aunt will hire me? What the—?"

"No! Well, not quite. Listen. I think the massage parlor is really a brothel. That's why Auntie doesn't let me go inside any of the massage rooms. I think some of the girls who work here are runaways, or drug addicts, or in trouble with the law. I think Auntie helps them, gets them off the streets, and then forces them to work for her to pay her back.

"If you dress up, look older, you can hang around outside and talk to some of these girls. Maybe they've seen your friend."

"Mèimei, that's brilliant." I jumped out of the chair and hugged her. "I'll find Emma now. I just know I will."

"Take it easy there, tiger. It's going to be dangerous for you. And you can't let Auntie see you. You can't just start asking questions right away, either. You'll have to earn their trust or they'll think you're an undercover narc."

"What's a narc?"

"Wow, you really don't know anything, do you?" Mèimei laughed.

I shrugged.

"Narc stands for narcotics agent, but it's also a police informant who works with the feds to bust drug dealers and hookers. If they even suspect you might *know* a cop, they won't go anywhere near you."

"Okay, don't act like a cop. Got it."

"V, this isn't a joke, you know—"

"I know. I'll be careful, I promise."

At that moment, my stomach rumbled so loud Mèimei thought I was dying. "Wow, girl. Don't you ever eat?" She laughed. "Stay here. I'll go in the kitchen and get us some food."

"Do you have any peanut butter?"

Mèimei gawked at me, wide-eyed, like I'd just announced I was from outer space.

I felt my cheeks flush as I said, "I always eat peanut butter when I'm nervous . . . or . . . any time, really. It's my favorite food group."

Mèimei laughed. "That's a good one, V. You had me going for a minute there." She put her finger to her lips, reminding both of us to be quiet, and left the room.

She came back about fifteen minutes later with an amazing-smelling feast of rice, noodles, and vegetables, but no peanut butter. It didn't matter, I was famished. Since I'd gotten up so early, I just realized I hadn't eaten since dinner at home, the previous night.

24

EMERGENCY SURGERY

I learned later that, while I was in the air on my way to Portland, my mom was at St. Joseph Hospital in Orange, California, in emergency surgery. The chemo wasn't working, her tumor wasn't shrinking, and they decided to do a double mastectomy earlier than planned. She hadn't told me what her test results had been . . . and I hadn't asked. It was probably better that I didn't know. Mom and Dad had purposely kept me in the dark so I could enjoy my little vacation with Aunt Karen. So while I was hatching a plan with Mèimei to find Emma, my dad was in a hospital waiting room a thousand miles away rethinking whether or not he should have told me about Mom's surgery before I left.

Carlos Jiménez paced in the lobby at St. Joe's, wondering if he should call his daughter. He checked his watch and realized V's plane wouldn't touch down in Portland for another hour, then he chastised himself for thinking her phone would work while she was in midair. His wife had just entered surgery, and they had decided not to tell the kids about it.

But now he had second thoughts. *What if Hannah doesn't wake up? What if something goes wrong in the OR? V will never forgive me. We shouldn't have let her go to Portland. I should have put my foot down. Can I even trust nutty Aunt Karen to take care of her? What was I thinking when I'd agreed to this trip?*

"Carlos, you're going to wear a hole in the floor," Gwen whispered. "Sit down and relax. There's nothing we can do right now but wait. Hannah is in good hands."

"Gwen, how can you be so calm? That's your daughter in there. She's fighting for her life," he insisted.

"Don't be so dramatic, Carlos. They're just removing a tumor and breast tissue. It's a relatively minimally invasive surgery. It's not like they have to cut her open and expose her organs. She'll be fine. Now, please sit down. Watching you pace about is making me dizzy."

Gwen was a no-nonsense person who didn't mince words. She'd been a nurse for forty years and had retired at 65. Two years later, she lost her husband, Hannah's father, to lung cancer. But his was different. His had been a silent killer. By the time the doctors discovered and diagnosed his condition, it was too late. He'd died two months later, barely enough time to get his affairs in order and say goodbye. That was only a year ago.

Carlos walked over and eased down into the chair next to his mother-in-law. He looked like he hadn't slept in weeks. He'd tried to keep it together for Hannah and the kids, tried to be brave, but it was eating away at him. His wife had cancer. His wife, the love of his life, the mother of his children, was in surgery getting her breasts removed. *Lopped off.* How had it come to this?

Gwen placed her hand on his knee. "She's going to be okay, you know."

"What makes you so sure? How can you say that with such certainty?"

"Because I have faith, dear. It's not her time yet. I know it. I pray day and night for Hannah, you, and the kids. God has filled me with a peace that goes beyond all understanding." She nodded her head and smiled, as if willing him to get it.

"I don't know, Gwen. You know we don't go to church much."

"You don't have to go to church to have faith, Carlos. God will meet you where you're at."

Carlos sighed. "Can we not talk about this right now? Please? I don't need a sermon."

"And I'm not giving you one." She patted his knee and reached into her bag, pulling out a red-and-black knitting project. She began to knit, and Carlos was strangely lulled by the soft clicking of the knitting needles.

Three hours later, in a chair at his wife's bedside, Carlos held Hannah's hand while tears of joy streamed down his face.

"Who died?" Hannah asked. She wiped a tear from his cheek, her own eyes welling up with tears that threatened to spill over. Blinking the wetness away, her eyes sparkled as she gazed lovingly at her husband and squeezed his hand.

"Not you, my love." He winked and kissed her hand. "These are happy tears. Come on, don't you know that real men cry?"

"Ahem, I hate to interrupt, but before you two get any mushier I have to take her vitals," a nurse said good-naturedly.

Carlos gently returned Hannah's squeeze, squared his shoulders, and stood up to let the nurse through. "I'll be right outside, babe." He walked out and closed the door behind him.

"Holy smokes, what I wouldn't give for a man to look at me

the way that man just looked at you. He's one handsome, tall drink of water. How long have you two been married?"

"Oh, we're not married. He's my illicit lover," Hannah joked.

The nurse's face flushed crimson, and she immediately turned away to check the monitor.

"Relax, I'm messing with you." Hannah smirked. "Sorry, I can be a bit of an imp sometimes. Carlos and I have been married for nearly sixteen years. Our anniversary is coming up December 28th, and I'm more in love with him today than I was then. He's my rock. He picks up my broken pieces and holds me together. He keeps me sane. He is the strongest person I know. He literally and metaphorically has carried me through the last month. How I ever deserved him, I'll never know. There has never been a more committed, loving human being or husband. I'm the luckiest woman in the world, and it is a great day to be alive."

25

A NIGHT ON THE TOWN

"Whoa, girl. I think you can pull it off." Mèimei whistled a sharp, shrill whistle. "At least you don't look 12 anymore. Ha ha ha!" She enjoyed the moment at my expense.

"Thanks," I replied curtly. "Now hand me more tissue. I've got an oversized bra to finish stuffing." I wore a tight, pale blue tank top, black miniskirt, black stockings, gold platform sandals, and enough makeup to supply an entire cheerleading squad. I felt like a circus clown, but Mèimei assured me the makeup was necessary. Other than elaborate Halloween costumes, this was the first time I'd ever worn makeup.

Mèimei curled my hair, teased it, and emptied nearly an entire can of hairspray on it.

"Is all this stuff really necessary?" I whined.

"You don't want them to suspect your real age, right? This makes you look older. Kinda trashy," she said, giggling, "but older."

"Gee, thanks." I studied my reflection in the mirror that hung over Mèimei's dresser as I adjusted my ill-fitting bra. I barely recognized my own image. I couldn't believe I was really going to go through with this.

Dressed like an actual prostitute, about to go out and talk to *real-life prostitutes* . . . I shook my head in disbelief. Did I have what it would take to pull this off? Could I be convincing enough to get these girls to trust me? Would they be able to tell me where Emma was?

I suddenly felt small and helpless as I contemplated the enormous task in front of me. Who did I think I was to fly up here and traipse around all over the streets of Portland, so far away from home, to find my friend and bring her back? Unsupervised.

My parents would freak out if they saw me now.

My phone sprang to life, blaring the tune "Daughters" by John Mayer. It was my custom ringtone for when my dad called me. Mèimei and I both jumped and stared at my phone, which I'd left on her dresser.

"Turn it off before somebody hears it!" Mèimei snapped.

I lunged for the phone and answered it without thinking. "Hi, Dad. What's up?"

"Hi, V. How's my favorite daughter?" Dad replied.

"Funny, Dad. Of course I'm your favorite *daughter* because I'm your only daughter—duh." I paused for dramatic effect and then asked, "But am I your favorite kid?"

"You know I love you both equally—"

"Yeah, yeah. It's the same answer every time," I teased. It felt good to hear his voice.

"How are you and Aunt Karen getting along?"

"Great! It's going great. She's in the kitchen making our dinner right now." I glanced at Mèimei, who looked about ready to explode. "Um, Dad? I have to go soon because dinner's almost ready and Aunt Karen asked me to set the table."

"Actually, V, there's something I need to tell you first."

"What is it?"

"Your mother was rushed into emergency surgery this morning. The chemotherapy didn't shrink the tumor and the oncologist thought it best to get it out of there now."

"What? Why didn't you tell me? Is she okay? Can I talk to her?" Tears sprang to my eyes.

"She's fine. She's a fighter. You know that. The surgery was a huge success. They were able to remove the whole tumor intact—they got it all. Right now, though, she's resting. Maybe you can call her tomorrow? I'll give you the direct number to her room at the hospital."

"Wow. I didn't think the surgery was supposed to happen for another two months. Not until after all the rounds of chemo were administered. I don't understand. How long have you known about this?"

"We found out yesterday when she got back her test results from the PET scan. The tumor hadn't budged—the chemo hadn't touched it. That happens sometimes, so they just needed to take the tumor now, before it got any bigger. We didn't tell you because we wanted you to have fun on your trip to Portland. We didn't want to worry you."

"But I should be there!" I sobbed.

"No, V. You shouldn't. You're a kid. Please, be a kid and have fun. Mom wants you to have fun. She has the best care possible; she's in good hands. Have a great weekend with Aunt Karen, honey. By the time you get home, Mom will be home, too. She only has to spend the weekend here and will be released from the hospital on Monday. Tell Aunt Karen hello for us, okay?"

"Okay. Wait. So . . . this surgery. Mom doesn't have any boobs anymore?"

Dad laughed. "Right. Mom is boobless."

We finished our conversation, and I set my phone down on Mèimei's bed, stunned.

A text came through. It was Dad texting me the number of the hospital so I could call Mom tomorrow.

"Turn it off." Mèimei's voice sounded far away.

"What?" I blinked at her.

"Turn off your phone. Or at least put it on silent. It makes too much noise."

"Oh. Okay." I picked up my phone and switched it to silent mode. "My mom got her boobs cut off today."

"I heard. I'm sorry."

"I feel so guilty."

"Why? You didn't give your mom cancer. You have no reason to—"

"I lied to her." I looked down at my feet, ashamed. I changed my voice to a whisper, barely able to say it out loud. "I lied to my parents about coming here. They think I'm visiting my aunt. They even bought my plane ticket. If they knew the truth . . ."

"They will obviously find out when you find your friend."

"*If* I find her."

"What? V, you can't give up now. Look how far you've come. What happened to brave 'Veronica Mars,' amazing teen detective, out to solve the big kidnapping case and get her friend back?"

"She's just a TV character, and I'm just a kid. This is real, Mèimei. And I don't know what I'm doing. Besides, I also feel guilty that I'm not at the hospital with my mom."

"Hmm. Would you rather be at a hospital watching your mom in bed, hooked up to tubes and IVs and crap, not able to do anything to help her? Or here, where you can make a real difference and find your missing friend?" She put her hands on her hips and glared at me.

"You're right," I agreed. But I couldn't meet her eyes. Instead, I walked back to the mirror and fussed with my bra again. It wouldn't stay in place. "And thanks for that lovely image you implanted in my mind. I don't want to see my mom hooked up to 'tubes and IVs and crap.' It will be better to see her at home when I get back on Monday. I mean, when I come back with Emma."

"That's the spirit. You're going to find her. I just know you will."

"Yep." I swallowed hard. "Now help me wipe this runny mascara off my face. I look like a freakin' raccoon."

Once Mèimei and I finished putting my face back together again, I took a final glance in the mirror, more resolved than ever to find Emma. I took a deep breath, glanced at Mèimei, and grabbed my phone.

"Let's do this." I turned and clomped out the door in my four-inch heels.

I STOOD on the corner in front of the Red Dragon massage parlor as frozen as a statue in the chilly October night. Mèimei couldn't do this with me; it was too risky for her if she got caught or was recognized. And if we were seen together, it would also blow my cover.

So, there I stood, all alone on a street corner, freezing my butt off and without a coat. I had tried to prepare myself for the many things that might happen tonight, like what I would say to the other girls, et cetera. But I absolutely was not prepared for the cold weather in Portland.

I took out my phone and checked my weather app. I had to

know what I was dealing with. I mean, I didn't want to die of hypothermia my first night in Portland.

The weather app mocked me. It read sixty-three degrees. *Are you kidding me?* Having lived in southern California my whole life, I wasn't used to a typical autumn. It was probably still eighty at home. So, for me, sixty-three might as well have been thirty-three, considering I felt practically naked.

A woman with shiny long black hair in a tight green minidress walked out of the massage parlor. She was pretty. I'd guess she was around 27 years old. She noticed me and smiled, then pulled a cigarette out of her purse and positioned it between her lips. "Gotta light?" she asked.

"M-me? Are you talking to me?" I stammered. *What an idiot! Pull yourself together, V.* "Sorry, no. I accidentally left my lighter on the table at dinner."

She laughed. "You're funny." She took the cigarette from her lips and placed it back in the cigarette pack. She then put the pack back into her purse. "I don't need it anyway. They say these things'll kill ya, ya know? Little cancer sticks." She laughed at her own joke.

She looked back over at me and said, "Hey, are you new? I've never seen you around here before."

I walked toward her as I was about to answer and nearly rolled my ankle, struggling to walk on my platform stilts. *Why did I let Mèimei talk me into getting these obnoxious shoes?*

"What's wrong with you? Can't you walk in heels?" she asked, laughing. "Yep, you're definitely new. Come here, new girl. What's your name?"

"My name?"

"No, your social security number. Yes, your name. It's okay, I don't bite."

"Um, my name is . . . my name is . . . Sandy."

"Sure it is, kid. Listen, the other girls aren't as nice as me, and they can spot a narc a mile away. So you better level with me. Who are you, and what are you doing here? You are clearly a fish out of water."

I studied her face and saw lines, signs of aging that caught me off guard. I changed my mind about her being 27. Maybe she was closer to 37? But she had kind eyes. She stared at me intently while I mulled over how much of the truth to tell her. I decided not to tell her quite everything just yet.

I cleared my throat, "My real name is Violet, but everyone calls me V. I'm here because I'm looking for my friend. We got separated a couple days ago at Pioneer Courthouse Square and I haven't seen her since. I thought she might be working down here."

"Hmm. Okay, I believe you, V. Besides, you're too young to be a narc. You're probably a runaway. Believe it or not, I was young like you once. All right, what does your friend look like?"

I pulled my phone out and showed her a picture of Emma. She said she hadn't seen her, and I was instantly deflated.

"Chin up, little girl. Just because I haven't seen her doesn't mean I'm completely useless to you. I know people. Besides, my shift just ended, and I'm in a good mood. I'm going to help you. Come on, I'll take you to someone who knows everything that happens around here. Follow me."

She took off walking at a brisk pace. I had to run to keep up —and that was no easy feat for a first-time wearer of platform heels.

We boarded a TriMet bus a few blocks away, headed toward another part of town. I tried to pay attention but was disoriented two right turns later. As we got closer to our stop, the girl in the green dress motioned for me to stand up and it occurred to me that I didn't know her name.

I grabbed on to the looped handle above my head to steady myself and asked her, "Why are you helping me?"

"Like I said, I was your age once. Someone helped me, so I'm paying it forward. By the way, my name is Sunny. I was born in South Korea and immigrated here with my parents when I was eight years old. But when we got here, they got really sick and died. I was placed in a foster home and ran away when I was ten. I've been on the streets ever since."

"Only ten? Wow. But . . . how did you survive? And you speak perfect English, without a trace of an accent. I don't understan—"

"An old English teacher sorta took me in. She was batty as hell and lived in a tent, but she taught me excellent English."

"But . . ."

Just then, three guys got on the bus and crowded behind us. The bus wasn't full, but they stood really close anyway. One of them whistled and groped my butt. The feel of his hand squeezing my rear end through my skirt made me nauseous. I froze—literally could not move. I just stared ahead at Sunny, afraid to move, or even breathe.

"Listen assholes, I have pepper spray and I know how to use it. Stay the fuck away from my friend or you'll be sorry," Sunny said as she reached into her purse.

"We ain't done nothin'. We're just lookin' for a little love. Isn't that right, sugar?" The same guy who groped me still had his hand firmly planted on my butt. He stood behind me and blew in my ear, clearly unfazed by Sunny's threat.

A tear slid down my face. I had no idea what to do. I felt completely powerless as I felt the guy's hot, rancid breath on my cheek. I closed my eyes and willed myself somewhere else. *Home.* I wanted to go home.

Suddenly, Sunny pushed me out of the way, kneed the guy in his nuts, and yelled, "Run!"

As the bus stopped, I ran off without looking back. The first guy screamed in pain while the other two laughed at him. I heard something drop and realized it was my phone just as the bus pulled away. I had shoved it in my bra because I didn't have a purse and I'd left my backpack at Mèimei's apartment.

"My phone!" I reached out toward the bus, but Sunny held me back.

"Let it go, V. It's not worth it. Those guys were gonna hurt you."

"Hurt me?" I repeated and glanced at her for clarification. When she didn't say anything, I realized what she meant. I vomited in my mouth a little and put my hand over my mouth to help me swallow it back down. Shaking my head, I whispered, "They'd do that to me on a public bus? I . . . I . . . I don't believe it."

"You'd be surprised what can happen around here."

"Oh my gosh! Sunny, you saved me. I don't think I could have lived through something like that."

"Yeah, don't worry about it. You're safe with me, kid. I was your age once, remember? Come on, we have to walk a couple blocks. It's not far."

She set out at a fast pace, and I hurried to follow after her. I knew we'd never talk about this again. I had a sinking feeling she'd probably lived through much worse.

"Sunny?"

"V?"

"Just how old are you?"

"19."

My jaw dropped.

"What's the matter, kid? I look like an old lady to you? Well, that's what nine years on the streets will do to you. I don't recommend it. Look, you don't have to tell me anything, but if you're a runaway . . . my advice? Make up with your parents and go home. The streets here will chew you up and spit you out. Believe it or not, I'm one of the lucky ones."

"Lucky ones?"

"Yeah, I had that old lady who taught me English looking out for me. She kept me off the drugs after I OD'd on heroin and almost died. She nursed me back to health, made sure I ate, and I got a second chance at life. Most girls like me get hooked on the drugs and never find a way out. But I'm saving up my money, and one of these days I'm going to get far, far away from this life."

26

MAMA AND SUNNY

Sunny and I walked in silence a while, each lost in our own thoughts. I couldn't imagine her life. I couldn't imagine how awful it must have been for her to lose her parents at such a young age, and for life with her foster family to be so bad that running away and living on the streets at the age of ten seemed like the best solution. I shuddered.

I have a good life. No, I have a great life! I have two loving parents, a sweet little brother, and my grandma. We have everything we need, like a roof over our heads, electricity and running water, plenty of food and clothes—things I've taken for granted my whole life.

I have old toys I've never played with, tons of stuffed animals, games, electronics, a comfy bed, and my own room. I'm spoiled! And poor Sunny never had any of that. She was robbed of her childhood—

"What are you doing?" Sunny sliced through the silence with her stern question, which sounded more like an accusation.

"Nothing. Wh-what do you mean?"

"I know that look, kid. You feel sorry for me. Let's get one thing clear, shall we? I don't need your pity. I can take care of myself, and I'm doing just fine. Now, close your mouth before I close it for you, and try to look like you're older than 12. Think you can manage that?"

I closed my mouth and nodded, afraid to say anything.

"Good, 'cuz we're here."

We approached an old brick building, went inside, and began walking up the stairs to the fourth floor. "Isn't there an elevator here?" I asked, slightly out of breath. Plus, my feet were killing me.

"Gee, why didn't I think of that?" Sunny rolled her eyes. "Got any more stupid questions, kid?"

"My name is V," I mumbled. I reached out for the handrail and kept trudging up without looking at her.

"What was that? Speak up, kid. This ol' lady can't hear you." Sunny laughed and slapped her knee.

"I just wish you'd stop calling me 'kid,' that's all."

"See, was that so hard? You just stood up for yourself, V. Well done." Sunny smiled at me. "Stick with me and you'll be a badass bitch that nobody can push around in no time."

We both laughed at that. The thought of me being 'badass' at anything was so ridiculous I laughed even harder.

A sharp elbow jabbed me in the ribs. "Ow! What did you do that for?"

"Quiet, they'll hear you," Sunny whispered. We reached the top of the stairs, and she added, "You need to let me do all the talking, even if you don't agree with what I'm saying. You just have to trust me. I know what I'm doing, okay?"

"Okay," I mouthed. We stood in front of apartment 4B, and my mouth went dry. I squeezed my eyes shut and summoned all my courage, including my inner 'badass.'

Here we go.

Sunny rapped on the door three times. We waited. She rapped three more times. We waited some more.

"What if nobody's here?"

"Shh. No talking, remember?"

The door opened two inches and a tiny girl with big dark eyes peered through the crack. "What do you want?"

"It's Sunny. We're looking for someone. I need to talk to Mama. Let me in."

The door opened wide. We walked in, but the girl was nowhere to be seen. Sunny turned and closed the door behind us.

"Sunny! Come give your Mama a hug. I've missed you." A thin, frail-looking Asian woman with black hair in a tight bun sat in a rocking chair in the dark. She had one hand on a fluffy gray cat dozing on her lap and the other around a cane.

"Hi Mama." Sunny strode across the living room and gingerly wrapped her arms around the woman in the chair. "My friend and I need to talk to you."

"Oh?" Mama glanced up at me. "Who's your friend?"

At this, a skinny boy wearing only jeans exploded into the living room and blocked my path before I had a chance to register anything. He looked about 13 and carried a machine gun, which he casually slung across his bare shoulder.

"It's okay, Han, she's with me." Sunny moved in front of me and put her hands up to ward off Han.

The boy relaxed but stayed in the room. He perched on the arm of the sofa and stared at me, practically never blinking. It was unnerving.

As my eyes adjusted to the darkness of the living room, lit only by the streetlights outside, I noticed Mama's right foot was severely disfigured. It appeared as though it had been mangled by an animal attack or something.

"Mama, this is my friend V. She's a working girl like me, and she's new in town. She and her friend rode in on a bus from Seattle a few days ago, but now she's lost her friend." Sunny threw a warning glance at me, but I didn't know why she was lying. She looked back at Mama and continued, "We're hoping you might have heard something that could help us track down V's friend."

"Seattle, you say?" Mama addressed me.

"Yes, ma'am." I fidgeted.

Great. I've never been to Seattle before and now I have to keep Sunny's lie going? I hadn't even told her where I'd come from. I guess she must have assumed Seattle, but—

"Ah, I love Seattle. Every time I visit, I always make sure to go up in the Space Needle. You can see the whole city from up there. And it's such a great draw for the tourists." She addressed me again, "Have you been up in the Space Needle, V?"

"No, ma'am."

"Well, why not? It doesn't cost a thing. You'd think it would be a big money maker, but they've decided to wave the admission fee and keep it free to the public. That is so generous of them. Don't you agree, V?"

I glanced at Sunny. She just shook her head. I cleared my parched throat and managed, "Yes, ma'am. When I find my friend and we go back home, we'll be sure to visit the Space Needle." But I couldn't look at her. Staring at the floor, my eyes inadvertently flitted to her mutilated foot.

Not missing a thing, Mama suddenly kicked her foot up at me and laughed.

Startled, I jumped and fell backward, landing hard on my butt.

Everyone laughed, even stone-faced Han with the gun.

Serious again, Mama leaned forward and locked eyes with me. "What happened to my foot is another story for another time. You, on the other hand, are lying to me. Why?"

I panicked and looked at Sunny. She quickly tried to smooth things over, by betraying me.

"Mama, she told me she was from Seattle when I met her. How was I supposed to know she was lying? How did *you* know she was lying? Anyway, she's harmless enough. Won't you just help us find her friend? Please?"

Mama looked from Sunny, to me, then back to Sunny. A smile slowly spread across her lips as she asked, "You wanna know how I can spot the lie? Easy. I tell my own lie first." She burst out laughing.

Sunny and I jumped at her shrill cackle.

Mama composed herself and continued, "The Space Needle charges an exorbitant amount of money for the privilege of riding up to their observation deck. *It has never been a free ride.* Anyone living on the streets anywhere near the Needle knows it's a giant tourist trap and ripe for the picking. I will not help you find anyone—not until you two start talking. And it better be the truth this time."

I was about to answer her when three loud raps on the door reverberated through the silence, causing me to jump again.

"You're so jumpy. What a scaredy cat," Han said. "Boo!" He laughed and shook his head.

The same tiny girl who had opened the door for Sunny and me darted out from a room down the hall. She unbolted the door and opened it a crack, "What do you want?"

"It's Pearl, you stupid idiot. Let us in!"

Tiny girl disconnected the chain-link latch and ran down the hallway again. I looked at Sunny quizzically.

"She loves to answer the door, so Mama lets her," Sunny whispered in my ear. "She's not right in the head. She was hit by a bus and left for dead. Mama took her in. Mama says she has a TBI."

"A TBI?"

"A traumatic brain injury. Shhh." She put her finger to her lips. "I'll tell you later."

Three girls crashed through the open door. One was bleeding and leaning on the other two. They didn't look much older than me.

"Jade's been shot. A pimp jumped us. Said we were on his turf. He pulled a gun on me, and Jade lunged at him. They struggled with his gun and it went off. Mama! You have to save her," one of the girls cried, I think it was Pearl.

"Han, bring me my black bag. Sunny, fill a large mixing bowl with water and get some fresh towels. Pearl, lay her down in the kitchen. And for God's sake, someone turn on some lights." Mama stood up with the aid of her cane and hobbled toward the kitchen while everyone else sprang into action.

Not wanting to get in the way, I stood in the far corner of the living room against the wall and watched the events unfold in front of me. I couldn't believe what was happening.

Mama lifted up her bad foot, leaned her cane against the counter, and stood on one leg. Then she gracefully sat down on the kitchen floor in one fluid movement. It looked like a trained dance or yoga move.

She tore open Jade's yellow dress and inspected the wound on her side, humming while she worked. No one else made a sound except for Jade's soft crying.

"You're okay," Mama soothed. "You can all relax. It's just a graze. Couple stitches and you'll be good as new in no time. No bullet. No hole. See?" She washed and sterilized the wound, then poured something on it so Jade wouldn't feel the needle when Mama sewed her up.

"Thank you, Mama!" Jade gushed. "You saved me!"

"Tsk, tsk. Hardly, dear. You're fine." She stood up and turned to Pearl and the other girl. "Do we need to worry about this guy? Did he follow you here?"

"No, Mama, we were very careful. Just like you taught us. We wouldn't lead anyone here," Pearl said.

"Yeah, we were careful. We ran down an alley and hid. We waited until we couldn't hear his footsteps anymore before coming here." The third girl beamed.

Mama turned on the third girl. "Did you stop and think that maybe he hid, too? Well, did you, Ruby?"

Ruby's smile turned into a frown and was replaced with a look of terror when a man appeared in the doorway. He wore a fitted black-and-white-striped suit, with a black shirt and tie and a fedora hat. He looked like a cross between a cartoon caricature and a gangster who had just stepped out of a 1920s-themed black-and-white movie. If not for the expression of abject fear on Ruby's face, I would have thought he was on his way to an elaborate Halloween party. He looked so out of place and comical to me, I actually suppressed a laugh.

"That's him!" Ruby screamed and pointed at the man standing in the entrance.

He hesitated only a moment before entering the living room, gun drawn and pointed at Mama. She was still in the kitchen and stood in front of the three girls. At that moment, I didn't know where Sunny, Han, or the tiny girl were, so I ducked down behind the sofa and peered around the side.

"Well, hello, Mama," the man said. "I wondered where you'd vanished off to. Figured I'd see you again sooner or later. How long has it been, hmm?" He smiled brightly—too bright.

His teeth sparkled like some of the rap artists I'd seen in music videos. I think they called it a bling grill.

"Danny." Mama stood tall and unwavering, an imposing force for such a petite woman with a lame foot. She held tightly on to her cane. "This is my home, and you are not welcome here. These girls are under my protection. I'm going to ask you nicely only once. Please leave."

"Mama, I'm hurt. Is that any way to treat your old friend, Danny Wu?" He waved his gun around. "Why don't you tell these young ladies how you and I met? Or how about how you got that repulsive, ugly, lame chunk o' meat that used to be a foot, huh?" He laughed a deep, sinister belly laugh.

The sound of his disturbing laughter reverberated throughout the apartment. It gave me chills.

Then I saw a fast flurry of movement out of the corner of my eye and turned to see Mama's cat race down the hallway and disappear. If I could, I'd run fast and far away, too.

A click drew my attention back to the scene in the kitchen. Han had the tip of his machine gun firmly planted in the middle of Danny's back.

"Like I said, Danny. I asked once, nicely," Mama said.

"Well, your boy's gonna have to shoot me then 'cuz I'm not leavin' until we settle this." Danny spun around and shot at Han.

He missed.

Han fired and yelled, "Yippee ki-yay, mother *feather!*" sending a spray of bullets into Danny's chest and stomach.

Danny fell. Dead.

27

ALIS VOLAT PROPRIIS

Han sat in Mama's rocking chair, blood spattered across his face, neck, and chest. Mama took the machine gun out of his trembling hands and asked Pearl to get a wet washcloth. She went back to the kitchen with the gun.

Han saw me, still crouched behind the sofa. He motioned for me to come out. "It's okay. Bad guy's dead. I killed him. First time I shot anybody. You know why I say 'feather'?"

I shook my head "no" but stayed where I was—in my hiding place.

"Because Mama doesn't let me say the other word. I saved Mama. I'm a hero. Just like Han Solo. My hero."

I thought Han must be in shock. I still hadn't moved. I glanced at the dead body on the floor maybe four feet away from me. I knew I was in shock, too.

"V?" Sunny's voice woke me from my dazed stupor. Where was she? Her voice sounded too soft, distant.

"V?"

I glanced around. I saw a foot sticking out from under the

side table that was next to the rocking chair. The table was covered with a turquoise silk tablecloth that reached the floor. It dawned on me that Sunny must have hidden under that table when I had hidden behind the sofa.

I crawled out of my hiding place and over to the table, staying on my hands and knees. I lifted up the tablecloth. Sunny sat under the table, leaning against the wall. Her hands and pretty green dress were covered with blood. I couldn't make sense of it. Why would Sunny's hands have blood on them?

"Sunny? You can come out now. He's dead. We're safe. Come out. Please," I pleaded.

"V. No. Listen." It seemed every word was hard for her to say.

I struggled to make sense of any of it. As if she could read my thoughts, she lifted up her right hand. Blood gushed out of the gaping hole her hand had covered up.

"Sunny! You've been shot! Mama—!"

"Shh. No time. Not safe. Listen. You can't stay here. V, *run.*" She reached out to me, but her hand fell back down.

No. That's not right. Why would her hand fall?

I pushed her shoulder. She slumped over. I shook her. She didn't respond. I tilted her head back and looked in her eyes. The light had gone out. Sunny was dead.

I bolted up and ran out of there as fast as my legs would take me, stopping only long enough to take off my worthless platform shoes and ditch them. I did not look back. Hot tears stung my cheeks as the cool night air dried them. I did what Sunny told me to do, her last words to me a command—I ran.

* * * * *

CLEARLY, running was not my thing. After only two blocks, my stockinged feet, already blistered from the platform shoes, forced me to stop due to their throbbing with pain from pounding the pavement so hard. I limped over to a tree, planted in the middle of the sidewalk, and puked out the contents of my insides onto the dirt. My retching turned into dry heaving until I was an empty shell. There was nothing left. My heart thudded in my ears so loud that I didn't hear the approaching footsteps behind me.

"Hey, there she is." The voice belonged to Pearl.

Taking Sunny's warning to heart about it not being safe, I chose to trust no one. I found the strength to stand up and run some more. I turned a corner and another one as fast as I could, hopefully losing my hunters. I was not about to become anyone's prey.

I needed to rest and get off my aching feet. I wandered aimlessly among the night people of the streets. No one paid attention to me, and I was good with that. But I was lost. And so very far from home.

I saw a "KEEP PORTLAND WEIRD" sign painted in big yellow letters across the back of a painted black brick building. I had seen the sign before, when I'd ridden the bus with Mèimei earlier that day. *Was that today?* This had been the longest day of my life.

I hobbled over to the building and collapsed onto the pavement underneath the sign. I sat with my back against the wall, a lone streetlight for company, and stared out at the parking lot.

As I sat there, I contemplated my fate. I pulled my knees up to my chest and wrapped my arms around myself to try to get some semblance of warmth. I let out a deep sigh and lost myself in my swirling thoughts.

Am I going to die tonight? Are they looking for me? Will they kill me? I've seen too much. I know too much. And Sunny. Poor, brave Sunny. Could this night get any worse?

First, some creepy guy puts his hands all over my butt. I lose my phone, I have no money, and I have no idea how to find Mèimei to get my stuff back.

I just saw two people die right in front of me.

And I'm no closer to finding Emma than I was when I got here this morning.

"And I really want my mom," I said out loud. I couldn't hold back the tears anymore. I cried and shivered and wondered if I might die right then from freezing to death.

Suddenly, a warmth enveloped me. A heavy coat had been draped over my shoulders. I looked up to smile at my angel, this wonderful creature who had come to comfort me. Instead, my eyes widened in fear.

"Relax," Han said. "It's okay. We come to help you. We're not the bad guys. Mama is not a bad guy. She takes care of all the kids on the streets. She sent me to find you, to take care of you. Come. We'll give you food and shelter, and get you cleaned up." He put his hand out to help me up.

Numbly, I put my hand in his and stood up. I put the coat on and zipped it up, grateful for its warmth.

Han and Pearl started walking away, expecting me to follow them.

I just stood still.

"Ugh. You ungrateful little brat. Do you know how long we've been out here searching for you?" Pearl said, rolling her eyes.

"If you're so good, why did Sunny tell me to run? Why did she say it wasn't safe?"

"See, Pearl? I knew it," Han said, grinning. He turned back to me and offered an explanation, "Sunny was confused. She got scared because Mama got stern with you. Mama helps all runaways, but she hates being lied to. She makes everyone tell the truth before she helps them. Mama would never hurt you or Sunny, but I guess Sunny didn't know that. Mama feels bad for what you saw. She wants to help you now."

"I don't care. I'm not going back to that place." I shuddered. "I'm not going anywhere with you two."

"Fine, have it your way. We couldn't care less." Pearl turned to leave.

"I'm sorry you feel that way, but it's a free country. We won't make you go with us." Han started to leave, but abruptly stopped and turned toward me again. "Hey, do you still want to find your friend?"

"Yes! Yes, more than anything."

"Check the Shanghai tunnels. Sometimes the bad guys catch girls and hide them in the tunnels before they move them to … um. Well, just be careful not to get caught, understand?"

"The Shanghai tunnels? Where can I find these tunnels?" I asked, hope filling me once again.

"They are next to the Portland Underground Tour in Chinatown, the part they don't let the tourists see. They're all boarded up, but everybody knows they're still being used. A few blocks that way," Pearl said, and she raised her arm to point over my left shoulder. "Just walk down Third Avenue and you'll see the sign for the tour."

When Pearl lifted her arm to show me which way to go, I noticed a cursive script tattoo down the length of her inner forearm. *"Alis volat propriis."*

"What does your tattoo say?" I nodded toward her arm.

"It's Latin. What's the matter, girl? Can't you read?"

"Be nice, Pearl." Han elbowed her.

"It means, 'She flies with her own wings.' Can we go now?"

Pearl put her hands on her hips and glared at Han. He nodded, and she stomped off ahead of him.

She flies with her own wings. I like that. I took a deep breath and watched them walk away until they disappeared around a corner.

With my new motto foremost in my mind, my 'What would Veronica do' mantra, and an inner resolve I didn't know I had, my determination to find Emma was stronger than ever. I wasn't about to give up now. I walked toward the Shanghai tunnels with renewed energy. I had a lead. Finally.

28

NEW SHOES

By the time I found the entrance to the Shanghai tunnels, which was linked to the Portland Underground Tour, it was three o'clock in the morning. Instead of plunging into the depths of darkness into an underground sea of cavernous tunnels, which in itself was intimidating enough, I forced myself to wait. Not only did I not have a flashlight, food, adequate rest, or warm clothing, I also didn't have a plan. As much as I wanted Emma to be down there and as much as I wanted to find her, I knew I wouldn't be any good to her without sleep and nourishment.

I managed to find some noodles and egg rolls in a dumpster outside a Chinese restaurant. I wolfed them down while trying not to think about what germs may be on them or what nature of food poisoning I might be subjecting myself to. I also found a hiding spot between two large planters on the side of a nearby bar. It would have to do. I huddled down and tucked my knees up into my chest and under my coat. I drifted off to dreamland, very thankful for my new coat.

"Kid. Hey, kid. Yoo-hoo. Yo, kid. Wake up!"

My eyes shot open to a smelly, dirty, unshaved face with no teeth inches from my own face. I tried to get up and run, but my legs were still tucked in my coat, creating a veritable straitjacket. I couldn't move.

Fear and panic flooded through my body like a tidal wave. "Please don't kill me," I rasped.

"What? You think I want to kill you? Oh, kid, I'm hurt." The dirty man backed away and stood up. "I may be a bum, but I'm not a scoundrel." He laughed at his joke.

"What do you want?" I tried to sound brave.

"I'm just wakin' you up 'cuz the cops patrol through here around nine to clear out all the vagrants. And guess what? It's nine. I'm just tryin' to be nice, keep you outta jail. That's all." His sad eyes flitted to the ground often as he spoke. He shoved a grimy hand in his coat pocket and brought out a roll of Life Savers. He took one out of the roll and offered it to me. "It's green. I never cared too much for the greens. Take it, kid. You'll be doin' me a favor, so I don't have to eat it."

Realizing I was no longer in imminent danger, my body relaxed. I untucked my legs and stretched them out. Then I reached out my hand and accepted the green Life Saver. "Thanks, I'll save it for later," I said, and put the candy in my pocket.

The man's mouth split into a wide, toothless grin. Just as he was about to say something, we heard angry shouts about a block away. He took off running in the other direction without hesitation. I jumped up and tried to follow him, but my foot was asleep. I had to shake it out and stomp on it a few times to get the blood circulating again. By the time my cold, shoeless foot felt normal, the Life Saver bum was nowhere in sight.

I trekked around the block to clear my head and come up with a plan as much as to get away from the beat cop. It was

Saturday morning, apparently after nine o'clock. I had been in Portland nearly twenty-four hours. Just one day. And I'd already witnessed two murders. But I had a lead on Emma. Now I just needed a plan.

But first, I have to pee!

I wandered toward the waterfront, hoping for a quiet, private area. Instead, I found street vendors setting out their wares, getting ready for 'Saturday Market.' But I also found porta potties. *Hooray for small miracles.*

As I pulled up my ripped, snagged stockings, I knew I looked awful. But what I really needed was a pair of shoes. I went back over to the outdoor market and tried to stay in the background as I combed the various artisan tables filled with homemade arts and crafts.

I spotted a table sporting rows and rows of white canvas tennis shoes that resembled Keds. They were hand-painted with multicolored designs and flowers. I watched the vendor set out more shoes as I planned how the heck I would manage to get myself a pair. The money my mom had given me before I left was in my backpack at Mèimei's apartment. I wanted to kick myself for not bringing any money with me. But then again, I hadn't planned on spending the night on the streets either.

As if by some magical force, the vendor suddenly turned around and walked away. I watched her until she disappeared, leaving her table unmanned. I couldn't believe my good fortune as I ran over to the table, scanned it, found sneakers my size, and mouthed "I'm sorry" to no one in particular. I grabbed the sneakers and stuffed them in my coat.

I walked as fast as I could, without calling attention to myself, back toward the tunnels, three blocks up. When I felt I had walked far enough away, I sat down on the sidewalk to put on the bright white sneakers. There were sunflowers and little white daisies, outlined in black, all over them. Not quite my thing, but they'd have to do.

Perfect fit! I couldn't remember how long it had been since I'd felt this happy about anything, even if I did have to resort to theft.

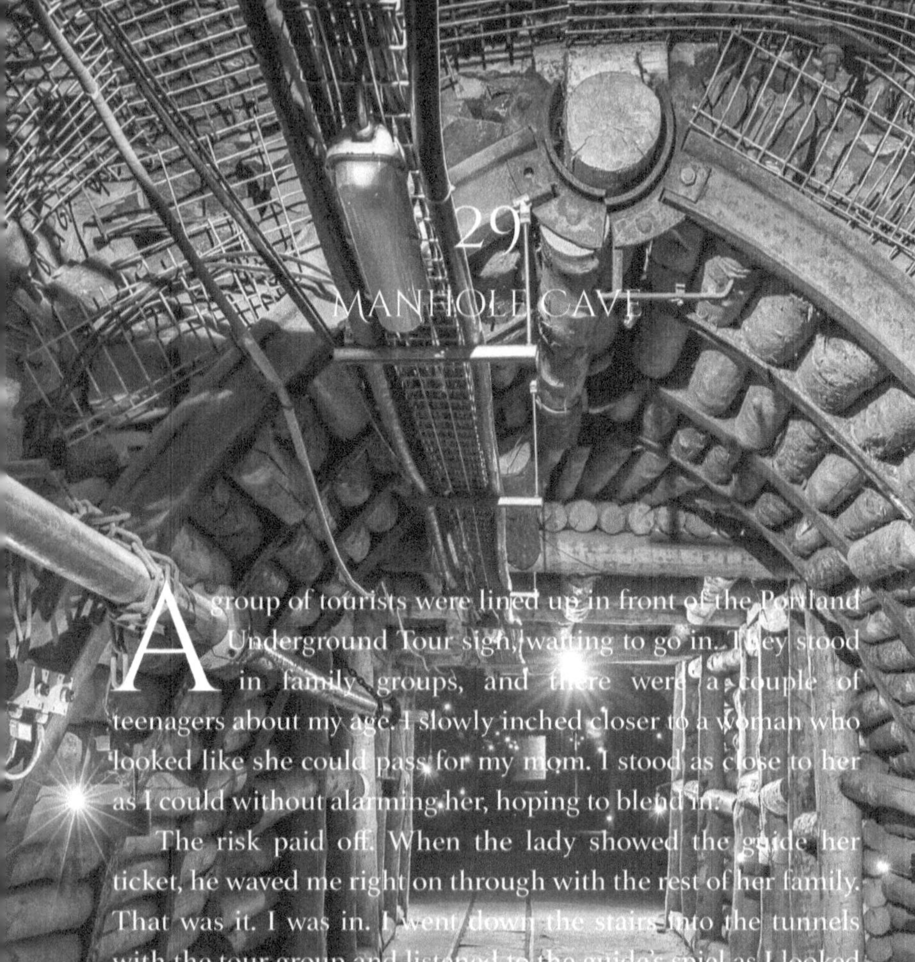

A group of tourists were lined up in front of the Portland Underground Tour sign, waiting to go in. They stood in family groups, and there were a couple of teenagers about my age. I slowly inched closer to a woman who looked like she could pass for my mom. I stood as close to her as I could without alarming her, hoping to blend in.

The risk paid off. When the lady showed the guide her ticket, he waved me right on through with the rest of her family. That was it. I was in. I went down the stairs into the tunnels with the tour group and listened to the guide's spiel as I looked for some sort of hidden passageway.

"Welcome to the Shanghai Tunnels," began the tour guide. "The tunnels before you were constructed in the 1860s. They connected the basements of the area hotels, bars, and a few shady businesses in Chinatown to the waterfront docks of the Willamette River. The Chinese built the passageways to move goods from the ships docked on the Willamette to the basement storage areas. This did two things: first, it kept the cargo clean and dry, and out of the wet and muddy weather; second, it avoided the streetcars and traffic of the bustling Chinatown above.

"Legend has it that this highly secretive labyrinth of connected tunnels, hidden stairways, secret panels, steel-barred doors, and many trap doors led to escape routes into far-off alleyways. And, they say, these tunnels were used for smuggling more than just cargo."

The tour guide stopped and waited for his audience to settle. His eyes pierced through us as he contemplated if we were worthy of hearing his secret. Then he waved his arms in the air in a broad, sweeping gesture to gather his flock in close.

"In fact," he whispered, "these very tunnels got their nickname for being used to 'shanghai' or *kidnap* drunken men by drugging them and forcing them to work on the ships! The captors would take these men through the tunnels to the ships and force them into slave labor by making them deckhands and part of the sailing crews. By the time they woke up from being drugged, they'd be in the middle of the ocean on their way to Shanghai, China. They'd better get to work or risk being thrown overboard—or worse!

"These days, however, there are many accounts of supernatural activity within these tunnels. Believers consider this area to be one of Oregon's most haunted sites. And if you want to hear more about that, we offer a special ghost tour after this one, so be sure to stick around for it."

He droned on with more myths and stopped at a few points of interest with staged old bunk beds and supplies in roped-off little rooms. I trailed behind, touching the walls as I passed, looking for secret panels. Just as I wondered if I'd know a secret panel if I came across one, something sprang back against my palm when I pushed on it.

I waited until the group was a good distance ahead of me

and pushed hard on the springy brick that blended in seam-lessly with the rest of the brick wall. This time, the brick slid out a little and then a small brick door swung open a few inches.

I bent down and squeezed through the opening. It was pitch black on the other side. I closed my eyes and counted to ten to adjust to the darkness. When I opened my eyes again, I could faintly make out the walls of a long tunnel.

Great. I just heard this place is freaking haunted, I can't see a thing, and now I'm in a dark tunnel by myself. Get a grip, V. You can do this. Crap. I hope there's no rats . . . or spiders, or ghosts, or—

CRASH!

"Aah! What was that?" I quickly realized I said that out loud, put my hand over my mouth, and held my breath. I put the other hand on the wall to guide me down the tunnel. I began creeping forward as quietly as I could, listening for more noises.

After I walked maybe fifty yards, I saw a beam of light under . . . a door? It was probably another secret panel. As I got closer, I realized it was an actual door, complete with a door-knob. *How odd.*

I turned the knob and pulled the door open, grateful it was unlocked. On the other side was a set of stairs leading down. *What, I'm not already far enough underground as it is?* I eased down the steps one stair at a time, straining to hear a sound, any sound.

I got to the bottom of the stairs and saw a short wall, or maybe some kind of partition or room divider. But it was no longer dark. *Is that daylight?*

I peered around the partition and saw a big room, like a cave with super high ceilings. When I looked up, I saw a round hole in the ceiling, like a skylight or something, only there was no glass window. It was just a hole, and I could see cloudy skies above. *A manhole? But there's no lid. So strange. I wonder where it leads.*

A movement to my left caught my eye. I turned my head and saw a giant cage, like a big dog kennel. My heart just about leaped out of my chest when I saw what—or rather, *who*—was inside.

* * * * *

I BLINKED RAPIDLY, wondering if I was hallucinating. It was just like my daydream, the one where I rescued Emma and Brylee from a cage, only it wasn't. This was real.

Two pairs of eyes stared at me from behind the bars. The girls' faces were in shadows, but I knew right away neither one belonged to Emma or Brylee. In fact, I had no idea if Brylee was even here. The Portland witnesses had only reported seeing Emma. Maybe they'd gotten separated and Brylee was still in California. I'd been so singularly focused on finding Emma, I hadn't even thought about Brylee until now. I hadn't thought about the possibility that she might be in Portland, too. I felt ashamed. But the truth was, I didn't know Brylee, and Emma and I had been best friends since first grade.

I glanced around the cage and saw four more girls inside, huddled together but unconscious. *Sleeping? Drugged?* I couldn't tell.

I ran up to the cage, and the girls at the bars hissed at me, "Shhh! They'll hear you. What are you doing here? Go away. You'll get us all killed," the first one said.

"I want to help you, to get you out of there," I said, looking straight into her haunted eyes. She looked emaciated. I guessed she was 16 or 17. "I'm also looking for my friend, Emma. Have you seen her?" My throat grew tight as I swallowed, anticipating her answer, hoping against hope that Emma was one of the four girls slumped in the corner.

She laughed, an eerily silent laugh, then squinted her eyes at me. "No," she spat out. "I haven't seen your friend. Now go away before they see you and lock you up in here with us. I don't want to share a cage with you." She slunk over to the far corner and turned her back to me.

I knew better than to argue with her and thought I'd try my luck with the second girl. But this time I tried a different tactic. "What's your name?"

"Jade," she whispered.

That got my attention. I moved closer to the cage. I stood inches from her face and saw the recognition in her eyes. "You were there. You were at Mama's last night. You'd been shot." My eyes flew to her side, but she was now wearing a thick sweatshirt and flannel pajama bottoms.

She looked down at my feet and then back up slowly. "After you left, Mama told Han and Pearl to go find you and bring you back. She said you'd seen too much. She wanted to talk to you, make sure you were okay. She gave me these clothes to wear and told me to rest. But I was scared. We all were. Mama said we had to help clean up the blood, had to help get rid of the bodies. But Ruby threw up, and Mama said we were worthless. She sent us to her storage locker downstairs for some heavy-duty trash bags, but we ran instead.

"I ran faster than Ruby, and when I stopped to wait, I looked back for her. I didn't see the van until it was too late. It stopped behind me, two men jumped out, grabbed me, and I blacked out. They must have hit me or something because I woke up in the back of the van with a headache. I didn't know how much time had passed, but I pretended I was still out. I heard them talking."

"Jade, I am so sorr—" I started to say.

"Be quiet," Jade cut me off. "No time. Listen to me. These men are very bad men. You don't want to mess with them, and you don't want to get caught. You can't get us out of here, but you can save yourself. Maybe you can go to the police and tell them we're here?"

"Of course I will."

"But first, listen. One of the men said he had to check on the new girls at the Red Dragon. He said they weren't from here. You're not from here either, right?"

"Right." I nodded, afraid to get too excited.

"I think your friend is there."

"At the Red Dragon? Are you sure? Mèimei's aunt owns it, but it's just a massage parlor."

"Look again. They hide girls there, too. Mama told us to stay away from that place."

"But Sunny works there. I mean, she did." I was confused.

The other girls stirred and began waking up. The first girl came back. "You got your answers. Now get out of here."

Jade nodded and said, "Yeah, you'd better go."

I still had so many questions to ask her, but I knew I couldn't risk getting caught. Reluctantly, I turned to leave. As I did, I whispered, "I'll get you out of here. I promise."

I wandered down Third Street looking for the Red Dragon massage parlor. By the time I'd found my way out of the tunnels, it was midday and sunny, not a cloud in the sky. *Well, Portland is full of surprises.* I shook my head in amazement. *I'm just glad it's not raining anymore.* I took off my coat and tied it around my waist.

I didn't have a plan, but in the twenty-six or so hours I'd been in this crazy town I'd made and lost two friends, nearly been attacked, lost my phone on a bus, watched someone get a bullet wound stitched up, and seen two people get shot and die right in front of me. And now I could add 'found six girls locked in a cage' to the list. I couldn't help it. I kept reliving and rehashing it all, trying to process everything but also trying to psych myself up.

Emma and Brylee could be in that massage parlor—locked up, scared, and in danger—right now. It was obvious the cops had no clue. Emma needed me more than ever—I was her only hope. No way was I going to let her down.

"Alis volat propriis. Alis volat propriis," I said out loud as I clenched and unclenched my fists. I stood in front of the Red Dragon massage parlor and took in a deep breath. "I'm coming, Emma. I'm flying in on my own damn wings, and I'm getting you out of there. I'm a badass now, just like Veronica Mars. I've stared into the face of death and lived through it. Nothing can stop me now."

Clap. Clap. Clap. Clap. "Nice pep talk. I see you survived the night."

I spun around and saw Mèimei grinning at me. "Mèimei!" I grabbed on to her and held her tight. "You have no idea. Boy am I glad to see you. You'll never believe the crazy night I just had. Wait till I tell you what hap—"

"V, you're choking me," she coughed out.

"Oh, sorry." I let her go and backed away a couple of steps. "We have to talk. I have so much to tell you."

"Okay, but not here. Auntie will see us. Let's go to the library."

"No, there's no time for that. Follow me." I walked a few steps and didn't hear anything, so I turned around. Mèimei just stood there gaping at me. "Hurry!" I snapped.

She looked surprised, paused for a second as if stunned, then ran to catch up to me. We jogged across the street to an alley out of sight of the Red Dragon. "V, what's gotten into you? You're, like, so bossy all the sudden."

"Like I said, I have a lot to tell you, but it will have to wait. What's important to know right now is that I think your aunt is hiding girls against their will—and I think Emma is one of them."

"What? No way." Mèimei looked at her feet, her tone unconvincing.

"I know you don't believe that. You've been suspicious for a while now, haven't you?"

She wouldn't look at me.

"You have to tell me what you know. Now. Lives depend on it. After the night I've had, trust me, you don't want to mess with me. I know she's your aunt, but she's putting girls in danger. You have to stop protecting her."

Nothing.

"Mèimei, please. I'm begging you. Emma's my best friend. She could die in there!"

Mèimei's head jerked up, and she gaped at me. *That got her attention. Good, she needs a wake-up call.*

Mèimei burst into tears and told me about the basement beneath the massage parlor. She said she sometimes heard crying and other strange noises coming from down there. Once she started talking, the floodgates opened up. I couldn't get her to shut up, but I needed to concentrate. I needed to figure out a way in, and a way to get Emma and Brylee out.

IT TURNED out that Mèimei knew a lot more than she'd been willing to tell me yesterday. Following her directions, I found a secret underground tunnel that took me directly to the basement under the Red Dragon across the street. It wasn't even guarded.

I pushed on a brick that eased open a secret panel, which resembled a brick wall just like the one I had stumbled across on the tour. I squeezed through the hidden half-door opening and wondered if it was still in use. I hoped against hope that I wasn't about to walk into a room filled with guards and guns.

I found myself in a dark, foul-smelling basement. It was just one big room. A faint light came from under a single door on the far wall.

On the floor were two rows of twin mattresses with varying colors of thin, worn blankets. And under the blankets? Sleeping shapes. There must have been about twenty. My heart thudded in my ears as I took in the scene.

I scanned the room quickly, searching for sitting or standing shadow people. To my surprise, the room was unguarded. There were only the sleeping people on the mattresses—and me. I wished I had a flashlight, or at least decent night vision. I hated walking around in the dark.

Sucking in my breath, I got down on my hands and knees so I could feel my way around better. I crawled over to the first row of beds and peered into the sleeping faces, looking for the one face that was forever imprinted on my heart.

The faces consisted of different races and ages, from teen girls to adult women. They hardly stirred as I passed.

When I crawled over to the eighth bed of the first row, I saw her. It was Emma. I'd know that face anywhere. I touched her cheek.

She didn't move. She slept as if dead. She must have been drugged.

Maybe they're all drugged? Maybe that's why no one's moving. They're too quiet. Crap! How do I wake her?

I put my lips next to her ear and whispered, "Emma."

Her eyes flew open. "V?"

We stared at each other for a millisecond. I put my finger up to my lips. She understood. I motioned for her to get up.

Carefully and quietly, she eased off the mattress. But instead of joining me, she stood up and walked over to the second row.

I pleaded with my eyes for her to stop, but she kept going.

She knelt down next to a mattress in the second row and woke up its occupant.

That person got up and silently followed Emma back over to me. It was Brylee, but she looked so different. I barely recognized her.

I motioned them to follow me, and I took them out the way I had come in, through the hidden panel. We crept down the tunnel collectively holding our breaths. No one said a word.

Only when we were out of the tunnel and back outside did someone finally say something. It was Emma.

"I knew you'd find us. Oh, V, I just knew you'd find us. I prayed every day, and I had a dream about this. And here you are."

"Emma, I never stopped looking for you. I knew you were alive. I knew I'd find you. I kept the faith." I hugged her, and we held each other for a long time, neither one wanting to let the other one go.

I peered over Emma's shoulder and glanced at Brylee. She stood motionless, with no expression, no joy on her face. With one arm, I reached out to her and pulled her over to us. We held on to each other, the three of us. Emma and I cried, but not Brylee.

A voice announced, "Wow, so you found her. That's awesome. I'm so happy for you."

Emma jumped.

I reluctantly let go of our embrace and turned toward Mèimei. "Yes, I found them! Thank you so much for all your help, Mèimei! I never would have been able to get them out of there without you." I turned to Emma and Brylee. "Guys, this is Mèimei. She helped me find you. She told me about the secret tunnel so I could get you out undetected."

"Hello." Mèimei waved.

"Hi," Emma said.

Brylee still hadn't spoken.

"You guys better get out of here before they realize you're gone," Mèimei said.

"She's right. I guess it's time to go now. Thank you, Mèimei." I gave her a big hug. Then I locked arms with Emma, and Emma held on to Brylee. The three of us began walking down the alley.

"Wait, I almost forgot," Mèimei called out. "Here's your stuff. And I put in some apples and some egg rolls, too, in case you were hungry." She handed me my bag, and my stomach growled at the mention of food. I reluctantly remembered my dumpster raid in the middle of the night, my crazy, terrible night—and that I hadn't had a chance to fill in Mèimei. It all seemed so long ago. But I couldn't tell her now. I had to get us to safety. We had to get out of there.

"Great," I said. "Thank you so much, Mèimei. I wish there was some way I could repay you. You've been so kind and helpful to me." I took my backpack from her and slung it over my shoulder. Now I had money for bus tickets to the airport. I figured once we got there I could call Dad and he'd get tickets for Emma and Brylee so we could all fly home. I couldn't wait to tell him I'd found them.

31
POLICE

We walked a few blocks over to Fifth Street to get on a bus that would take us to a transfer station where we'd hop on the MAX train that would take us to the Portland airport. I could barely contain my excitement that I'd found Emma and gotten her out of there so easily. I figured once I got us to the safety of the airport, I'd call the police and tell them where all the other girls were. I could even use the anonymous FBI tip hotline if I wanted to stay out of it. At this point, I was exhausted. I just wanted to go home and forget about this nightmare of a trip. I just wanted our lives to go back to normal again.

I was so happy to have my Emma back. I noticed she and Brylee acted odd, but I figured they were probably still in shock or something. I mean, they were sleeping in a basement in the middle of the day. I couldn't imagine what they'd been through. And frankly, I didn't want to.

We rode the bus to Northeast Portland, where we got off and transferred to the Redline MAX light rail. As soon as we boarded the MAX train and sat down, two police officers also boarded and headed straight toward us.

"Violet Jiménez? Are you Violet Jiménez?" The first officer looked expectantly at me.

I looked around for an escape. The second officer blocked my path.

I looked up at the first officer. "I am," I said, determined not to show fear.

"Ladies, I'm going to have to ask you to step off the train and come with us," he said.

"What? Why?" I asked, incredulous. "We didn't do anything. You can't just arrest us without cause."

"Sorry, Miss Jiménez, it's for your own protection. All will soon be explained to you. Now, please get up and follow us. Come on, let's go."

Emma and Brylee were scared and looked to me, their rescuer, for help. I didn't know how the policemen knew my identity and was pretty freaked out myself. But I decided to cooperate with them—as if I had other options—and we got off the MAX train. They escorted us to a police car and asked us to get in. When I protested, they assured us that we were not under arrest. The three of us climbed into the back seat and rode in silence to the police station.

When we got there, they placed us in a holding cell without explanation. No one said a word to us. I was confused and beyond pissed. I knew I had rights. If I demanded the phone call I was entitled to make, who would I call? Emma and Brylee huddled together in a corner of the cell in silence while I paced. They must have still been under the effects of the drugs that made them sleep in the middle of the day, or in shock that they'd been rescued, or something. But I didn't want to think about the 'or something' part.

I needed to know why we were locked in a cell for no reason and why no one would talk to us. After about twenty minutes of pacing and trying to get someone's attention, Lomeli showed up and asked a police officer to open the cell and let us out. *What the heck?*

"Detective Lomeli, what are you doing here?" I shouted, not sure whether to laugh or cry.

"Well, V, I suppose I should ask you the same thing," Lomeli shot back. "Are you going to introduce me to your friends, or did you also leave your manners behind when you lied to your parents, hopped on a plane, flew to Portland, interfered with an FBI criminal investigation, and just about got yourself killed?"

Ignoring his accusatory tone, and not wanting to face that I was possibly in trouble, I smiled and said, "I'd be happy to. Detective Lomeli, this is Emma Moreno, my best friend since first grade. And this is Brylee Rossi. I single-handedly rescued both of them from the basement of the—"

"That's enough, V," Lomeli said and held up his hand. "Let's go somewhere more comfortable where we can have a nice long chat, shall we? But first, let's get your friends taken care of."

THREE HOURS LATER, I sat in an empty conference room sipping my first cup of coffee as I waited for Emma and Brylee to be brought in. Truthfully, I thought the coffee tasted bitter, and I failed to see the appeal. Maybe it was an acquired taste and it would grow on me, but I doubted it.

I wore a matching navy blue sweatshirt and sweatpants emblazoned with "PPD," for Portland Police Department, and my white tennis shoes with the painted daisies—quite the fashion statement. Thankfully, they'd let me change out of my ridiculous skimpy costume with the snagged tights and Sunny's bloodstains, which they collected for evidence.

When they'd handed me the sweats, they had also let me go into the bathroom and freshen up a bit. I didn't recognize the girl I saw in the mirror staring back at me. She was so far from the fresh-faced, wide-eyed girl I'd been two days ago. *And I'd kill for a shower right now. Hmm, maybe a poor choice of words.*

I'd scrubbed off the makeup the best I could, using my hands and the liquid hand soap near the sink. I ran my fingers through my hair, wiped out my armpits with wet paper towels, and decided to call it good enough. For some reason, the police took my backpack when I got there and they still hadn't given it back to me. *I don't know what they think they're going to find in there but not my phone, that's for sure.* I sighed. What a crazy thirty-six or so hours it had been.

After freshening up, I'd told a conference room full of FBI agents, a few police officers, and Lomeli everything I knew about the tunnels, the girls I'd found in the cage, the Red Dragon's basement and the twenty girls there, Mèimei's aunt, and even about Danny Wu, Mama, and Sunny's tragic death.

I'd drawn detailed maps, the best I could, of the tunnels to the secret doors and panels, the cage under the manhole skylight, and the basement under the Red Dragon. I'd also told Lomeli about Mrs. Lee and her grandson, and how I'd pieced it all together.

While I'd been busy telling law enforcement's finest how I'd cracked their case wide open, Emma and Brylee had been quietly whisked away. Lomeli said they were talking to a psychologist or something and that they'd meet me in the conference room when they were through.

They'd let Emma call her mom, and I called Dad, but

Brylee didn't want to call anyone. Dad sounded mad and glad, and relieved about Emma, all at once. Once he calmed down, he cleared up the mystery around Lomeli's sudden appearance in Portland.

Dad told me that when he'd talked to me last night I sounded kind of funny. He called again an hour later because Mom had woken up and wanted to talk to me. When I didn't answer my phone, he'd called a bunch of times and had finally called Aunt Karen. Naturally, she'd told him I wasn't there and never had been, and no, she didn't have tickets to see Kristen Bell, and no, she hadn't written any letter inviting me to Portland for the weekend.

From there, Dad had quickly figured out that I was really looking for Emma. He called Lomeli and told him what I'd done. Lomeli immediately contacted the Portland Police, then got on a plane to track me down and save me from myself.

32

GOING HOME

We were finally released into Lomeli's custody for a late-night flight home. Emma, Brylee, and I each had a row to ourselves so we could lay down and get some sleep. Only, I couldn't sleep. My stomach hurt, but it wasn't like any stomach pains I'd ever felt before.

I got up to use the airplane's bathroom and discovered blood in my underwear. *Are you kidding me? Now?! After all I've been through, I have to get my stupid period now? Unbelievable.*

Not sure what to do since I hadn't had that talk with Mom yet, I pushed the flight attendant call button. I was beyond mortified.

I heard a knock at the door. "Do you need assistance, miss?" asked a female flight attendant.

"Um, you could say that," I said through the closed bathroom door. "I just got my period."

"Oh, okay. There are sanitary napkins for your use in the little bin in the wall next to you. Do you see it?"

I opened the door and poked my head out. "Yeah, I found it, but I don't know how to put it on."

She gave me a blank stare.

"This is my first period," I clarified.

"Oh! Oh sweetie, it's okay. There's nothing to be embarrassed about. All us girls get 'em. Putting the pad in place is easy. There's a little adhesive strip you need to pull off first. Here, let me show you."

The very nice flight attendant helped me get everything situated and then suggested I take my sweatshirt off and wrap it around my waist. I told her I wasn't wearing a shirt under it and shrugged, not wanting to have to explain everything. She had me stay there and said she'd be right back. It occurred to me they never gave me back my backpack and that these were the only clothes I had right now. I didn't even have the coat that Han had given me.

Great. I've got a freaking bloodstain on the backside of these sweats and nothing to cover it with.

The flight attendant returned with a gray T-shirt and said I could have it. Apparently, she'd gotten it out of her own personal overnight bag and given it to me. I gratefully took the T-shirt, put it on, wrapped the sweatshirt around my waist, and walked down the aisle back to my seat.

Just then, Emma popped her head up and grinned at me. "No way!" she said. "You finally got it?"

"Got what?" I replied. "Emma, I have no idea what you're talking about."

"Ha! You're not fooling anyone with the ol' 'sweatshirt wrapped around the waist' trick. Take it off and turn around. Let me see."

"No, gross! Now shut up before you announce it to the whole plane," I whispered in mock anger. "Or do I need to remind you how you hid in the bathroom stall in the girls' locker room when you got your first period, and you wouldn't come out until I gave you clean clothes to change into?"

Emma made a face and stuck her tongue out at me.

The truth was that was the first time I'd seen her smile or joke around since I'd rescued her. It gave me hope.

It was four o'clock in the morning on Sunday by the time Dad and I got home. He and Rosa were at the airport to greet us. Brylee's mom was there, too. It had been so good to see everyone, to have Emma back, to be reunited. But now I was exhausted. All I wanted was to take a shower and sleep for about twelve hours straight.

But that was not to be. Dad knocked at my door at noon and said Detective Lomeli needed me down at the station as soon as I could get there. I guess there were a few matters to attend to before we could wrap up this case and go back to our normal lives.

An hour later, I sat in the chair next to Lomeli's desk, waiting for him to get out of a meeting. Boredom and curiosity getting the better of me, I snooped around a little. I found a file labeled "Chiang Wu" under a stack of papers and picked it up.

Chiang Wu, now 80 years old, was a Triad boss in Los Angeles. He had an extensive rap sheet of criminal activity and was a known drug smuggler and money launderer. The Triads were part of an international organized crime syndicate, blah, blah, blah. I started skimming the file because I wasn't sure how this pertained to Emma and Brylee's kidnapping. And then I read it, something that connected the dots for me. I almost dropped the file.

"Chiang Wu and Ji-yeon Lee, 78, Orange, CA, are the parents of Danny Wu, 43, Portland, OR, deceased." *Mrs. Lee was Danny Wu's mother? The thug that Han shot in front of me?* I tried to process that information as I looked down at the file again.

"A little light reading there, Miss Jiménez?" Lomeli was back.

Uh-oh. Busted. I put the file down and turned to face him.

"No, by all means, keep reading. I think you'll find it *very* interesting, V."

"You left it for me, didn't you? You wanted me to read this?" I asked, not sure what to think.

"Yes, V, I *wanted* you to read it. You interfered with a—"

"Mrs. Lee is Danny Wu's mother? What about her grandson?"

"Hmm, didn't read very far, did ya? I should have stayed out longer. Look, kid, I don't have time to play connect the family tree with you. You have your friends back, so how about we—"

"But if Danny Wu is her son, then that means—"

Lomeli sighed. "So we're doing this? You're not gonna leave until I decipher this for you?"

I shook my head.

"Right. Okay, pay attention. Mrs. Lee married Mr. Lee and they had a healthy strapping boy they named Sam. Sam grew up, married, and had a son he named Kenny. Kenny is the 36-year-old grandson of Mrs. Lee and the one who kidnapped your friends, among other things. Kenny's father, Mrs. Lee's son, is clean as far as we know. It seems Mrs. Lee got into the Wu criminal family business after her husband's, Mr. Lee's, untimely death—deemed a mysterious 'accidental' drowning—six years ago.

"When little Sammy was II, Mrs. Lee met and had an affair with Chiang Wu. Nine months later, baby Danny Wu was born.

Chiang took the baby away from Mrs. Lee so he could groom him to take over the Triads one day, since Danny was his only heir, even if illegitimate.

"Danny never married or had children, so he leaned on his nephew, Kenny, to help run things. Danny's cousin, Zhang Xiu Wu (you know her as your friend Mèimei's 'Auntie') ran things in Portland with her sister. The sister (Mèimei's mother) was killed by Wu's men two years ago, and Auntie was forced to take in Mèimei and her brother, Qiang. It was Mèimei's mother's dying wish that Mèimei never become part of the business. But Qiang was already involved by then, so his fate was sealed."

"And the business that Mèimei's aunt ran?"

"A sex trafficking ring from four massage parlors in Portland."

"Sex trafficking?" I couldn't believe what I was hearing. I guess that accounted for the twenty girls and women I'd seen sleeping on the mattresses in that basement.

"Yes, V, sex trafficking. As I was trying to tell you earlier, you interfered with a major sting operation, according to the FBI. They've been investigating and closely monitoring the Wu family and the Triads for months between Orange County, Los Angeles, and Portland. Due to the Wu family's ties in Portland, they infiltrated the massage parlors and turned them into brothels. They've kidnapped hundreds of young women, runaways, and teenage girls and sold them into modern-day slavery and prostitution. But because of you—"

"But you arrested them. Everyone's been arrested, and Danny Wu is dead, and Emma and Brylee are home safe, and those twenty or so others, and . . ."

"When Zhang Xiu Wu and her nephew, Qiang, were taken into custody and the Red Dragon was forcibly shut down, the other parlors got wind of it and relocated. Vanished. All our leads dried up."

"But we saved those girls. Doesn't that mean anything?"

"Sure it does. We saved twenty-six—but we want to save them all."

"I am so sorry. I only wanted to help. I only wanted Emma back."

"I know you did, V. But you need to know that you can't go running around on some crime-solving spree without realizing the consequences of your actions. First of all, you're a kid. Secondly, you broke all kinds of laws. And thirdly, you almost got yourself killed—more than once, from what I heard. Leave the investigating to the police from now on, got it?"

"Yes, sir. Is that why you called me down here, to lecture me?"

"Don't get cute with me, young lady. You're the one who snooped around my desk and read a top-secret police file." He shook his head and added, "I really only called you in here to give you this." He reached down under his desk and pulled out my backpack. "Apparently, it got mixed in with police evidence. The Portland police thought you might want it back."

"Thank you," I said as I took the backpack from him.

33

PINKTOBER GIRL

Nearly four weeks later, Emma, Brylee, and I sat in the stands at our rally. It was Friday, October 30th, and my mom was once again in the spotlight, center stage, because she'd just won the staff's annual Halloween costume contest. What was she dressed as? Pinktober Girl, naturally.

But before I tell you about today's rally, I should probably give you a quick recap of the last four weeks.

Scotty and I went with Dad to pick up Mom from the hospital the day after I got back from Portland, the day I was actually supposed to return (Monday). We smoothed everything over with Aunt Karen, and of course, I had some major apologizing to do all around.

Mom didn't look as different or as strange as I thought she would, you know, on account of not having breasts anymore. She wore loose-fitting T-shirts and necklaces with big pendants, and I thought she looked great. Everyone said her surgery was a super success and that they got all the bad cells and cancer out. That was a huge relief. I was so happy to hear that my mom's cancer was gone! I guess she still has to do a few more radiation treatments, but she assured me it's only for 'insurance' and that she's totally fine.

Emma and Brylee had become close since they'd been in captivity together. I knew they'd been through a lot, and I couldn't even imagine everything that had happened to them, but I admit I was a little jealous. Emma didn't want to hang out with me like we used to. And the few times that we did hang out, she asked if Brylee could come, too. At first, I didn't like hanging out with Brylee. She didn't say much. But Dr. Sykes told me to be patient with both of them. She said they had been through so much that they had post-traumatic stress disorder (PTSD) and that they'd need extensive counseling and therapy to help them through it. She reassured me that they would heal, but that it would take time.

She also said I needed counseling and I bristled.

"Why? I wasn't kidnapped!" I snapped.

"No, but you saw two people die, V," she said. "That's not something that happens every day."

"I'm fine. Stop worrying about me and take care of Emma and Brylee."

"V, you're not fine. And that's okay, it's nothing to be defensive about. With counseling—"

"I don't need counseling." I crossed my arms for emphasis.

"Hmm, well then, how about you work on that temper?"

Okay, maybe she had a point.

MOM WENT BACK to work three weeks after her surgery. Everyone was surprised to see her back so soon. Dr. Fitz had told her to take the whole month off, but she just couldn't stay away. People kept asking her so many questions that she had to post another one of her health updates on her social media and blog. I was proud of this one. *Go Mom!*

October 28, 2015

It has been a busy Pinktober! A double mastectomy and some fabulous news from my surgeon, Dr. McAdams.

Everyone asks if I still have to do radiation even though my scans and biopsies came back clear. The answer is a big resounding YES. Stage four is stage four. We have known from the beginning that the medical community says I can't be "cured." My most recent PET/CT scan was completely clear, but because there is no possible way to know for sure if there are any cancer cells left in the areas they didn't biopsy, I have to continue with the radiation. It's like extra insurance. But the two areas where they were capable of doing biopsies from the surgery, the breast tissue and the lymph nodes under my left arm, came back 100 percent negative. That is AMAZING.

The surgeon even mentioned "Divine Intervention"—my jaw dropped. I pretty much skipped out of his office ready to take on the world! I couldn't stop smiling for three days, and we remain positive and hopeful for everything the future brings. With research and new clinical trials developing continually, cancer is becoming more like a chronic condition that can be zapped out if it ever comes back. So now I head into an aggressive course of radiation starting in November. Bring it.

I'm getting used to my new "boyish" figure—it's very strange—but I'm embracing it and adjusting. Carlos and the kids continue to be wonderful about my continually changing appearance. The newest development is the fuzzy, dark red hair that's sprouting up on my noggin. I have to say I'm relieved it isn't gray! There's only so much a girl can take.

I finally took some time off from work (I was politely threatened by various people, including Dr. Fitzgibbon, my principal). However, that didn't stop me from showing up at the Sierra vs. Orange High's football game the Saturday night after my surgery to see the Warriors clinch a victory in the final seconds! And it was a stadium packed in pink! What a joy to see our team playing their hearts out on the field—they rocked.

I'm back to work this week and LOVING it. My students make me smile every single day. I'll continue to post updates as I progress through the next treatments.

Love to all,

Hannah

WELL, that catches us up to today's rally. This morning, when Mom was trying to come up with a last-minute costume idea, I told her she should just be "Miss Pinktober Girl." She didn't immediately warm up to the idea, but then we remembered a T-shirt a friend had given her recently as a gag gift and everything fell into place. It was perfect.

Her wig was made of hot pink, long straight hair. I helped her brush it into two loose pigtails to wear in front. We added pink false eyelashes, and even pink eyeshadow, lipstick, and nail polish. But what made the costume a winner? It was her black T-shirt. Across the front, in large pink lettering it read,

"Heck yes, they're fake. The real ones tried to kill me." We taped balloons under the shirt, onto her chest, and she looked bustier than Pamela Anderson.

When my mother, Hannah Jiménez—or Mrs. J as the students called her—walked out at the rally and stood before the crowd, she received a standing ovation. Everyone was on their feet cheering and happy and celebrating. My mom positively beamed.

I looked around and saw that Emma and Brylee were clapping and cheering, too. It was the first time I'd seen either one of them truly happy, much less participating in a school function. My eyes met Emma's and I could tell her spark was back. At that moment, I knew she was going to be okay—and I beamed, too. After all, with my mom going into remission and my best friend back, I had plenty to celebrate.

As I walked toward the parking lot with Emma and Brylee after the rally, we heard a loud "pop" and my mom's shrill scream. She was a few feet ahead of us so we ran up and saw her sprawled on the sidewalk with some guy hovering over her.

"Mom? What happened? Are you okay?" I knelt down to help her up and pushed the guy out of the way so I could get to my mother. But then I turned on him. "Who are you?" I demanded.

"I'm so sorry. I was on my skateboard and I didn't see her there and we just kind of collided and—" he stammered.

"You stupid idiot! Do you have any idea who you just ran into?" I raised my arm and clenched my fist. He just stood there with a dumb expression on his face so I pulled my arm back and got ready to—

"V!" Mom looked panicked. "It was an accident. You're not going to hit him, are you?"

"I, uh, no, of course not, Mom." I unclenched my fist and

dropped my arm, embarrassed. I shook my head to clear it then helped Mom up off the ground while skateboarder guy, Emma, and Brylee stared at me.

"What are you all staring at? I'm fine. I'm not the one you should be worrying about. Come on, Mom, I'll take care of you. Are you hurt?"

"No, sweetie, I'm fine," Mom said.

We walked to her car and she looked down at her chest as she opened the passenger door for me.

"Crap!" Mom said.

"What?" I demanded, immediately concerned.

"That kid popped my balloon boob." She looked at me and winked. Then she sighed dramatically, reached under her shirt, and pulled out the second balloon. "We better pop the other one, too, so I'm not lopsided."

Leave it to Mom to lighten the mood. I laughed, in spite of myself. We all laughed. And it felt good.

While Emma and Brylee's story is a work of fiction, Sharmel's is not. The fictional Dr. Sykes's retelling of the abduction and murder of her friend Sharmel is based on the real life tragic case of Charmel Ulrich—a beautiful, vibrant life cut short—my friend. I hope this story honors her memory and helps people to remember the kind and radiant person she was. A portion of the proceeds from *Glass Stars* sales will be donated to the National Center for Missing and Exploited Children, in Charmel's name.

If you think you've seen a missing child, or for more information, go to missingkids.org or call 1-800-THE-LOST (1-800-843-5678).

More than one million children are victims of commercial sexual exploitation each year. If you or someone you know needs help, call the National Human Trafficking Hotline at (888) 373-7888.

THANK YOU

Would you like to read the story that Scotty's mom tells him at bedtime? It's called, "The Legend of the Glass Stars." You can download it for FREE by visiting my website and signing up for my newsletter. As a thank you for reading *Glass Stars* you'll also get Brylee's short story, "Running in the Rain" as well as updates on new releases. Just go to my website at taschelaine.com (click on the image for ebook).

If you enjoyed this book, I'd like to ask you for a favor. Will you please post an honest review for *Glass Stars* on Goodreads, Amazon, or your favorite bookstore or review site? A review is the best gift you could give an author. Thank you so much!

About the Author

Tasche Laine has worked as a journalist, teacher, and book editor. Her published works include book award winners *CLOSURE: based on a true story* and *CHAMELEON:* a domestic thriller; two short story anthologies: *Winds of Winter* and *Wings of Prophecy*; a Young Adult mystery series, *CHRONICLES OF V*; and the *Lil Peter* children's book series she co-writes with her husband, Peter.

She grew up in a small town in Oregon, has lived all over the U.S., and currently resides in the Pacific Northwest with her husband and puppy, Story. She also visits family in southern California as often as possible. For more information, please visit her website at taschelaine.com.

facebook.com/TascheLaine

instagram.com/tasches

amazon.com/author/taschelaine

goodreads.com/tasche_laine

bookbub.com/authors/tasche-laine

BRIGHT STARS

Book Two in the CHRONICLES of V series
coming soon!

A Driver's Ed scandal. Family issues at home. V is on the case again, even if it is just to get out of the house.

V is fifteen and can't wait to learn how to drive. But her parents are too busy with their own problems to bother to teach her. So when a guy at school tells her about a new driving school, she doesn't hesitate to sign up even if it sounds shady. When a slew of break-ins occur in her neighborhood, and the Driver's Ed teacher might be behind it, V is asked to call on her novice detective skills once again.

Now that her mom's cancer is in remission and her best friend is back, will V be able to live a normal teenage life? Or will she get in over her head, sucked into a case beyond anything she could possibly imagine?

Bright Stars picks up a year after *Glass Stars*, in the Chronicles of V, a young adult contemporary fiction series. If you like gutsy teen detectives, à la Veronica Mars or Nancy Drew, you'll love Tasche Laine's page-turning adventure.

Acknowledgments

The term "it takes a village" truly applies here. Without the help, guidance, insights, and support of the following people, you would not be holding this book in your hands right now. I'd like to acknowledge and thank them here.

First of all, thank you to my amazing editor, Allison Rose, of Purple Rose Editing. I am grateful for her eagle eye and ability to spot the tiniest of errors. Next, a big thanks goes to my talented cover designer over at 100 Covers (100covers.com).

And of course, I want to thank my early readers and two biggest fans, Kim and Tiana (my mother and my daughter)! Your valuable insights and support mean the world to me. Thank you both for reading everything I've ever written and continuing to cheer me on. Your love and encouragement have kept me bolstered and have allowed me to continue on my author journey during these trying times. As Hannah says, "I love you to the stars and infinity—forever!"

Thank you also to my beta readers whose helpful feedback and typo-catching is most appreciated: Kristi, Erin, Tina, Ken, and Elizabeth.

A very heartfelt thank you goes to Curt Ulrich and his family for allowing me to tell Charmel's story. Curt was instrumental in my fact-checking, and he answered my questions with grace and candor. Even though Charmel has been gone forty years, the pain and grief of her loss still feels very fresh.

Finally, to you the reader. Thank you for going on this adventure with V and her friends & family. I hope you'll join V on her next big case. Stay tuned for *Bright Stars*, the next book in the Chronicles of V.

ALSO BY TASCHE LAINE

CLOSURE: Based On A True Story

CHAMELEON: A Domestic Thriller

SHORT STORY COLLECTIONS

WINDS of WINTER

WINGS of PROPHECY

CHRONICLES OF V

GLASS STARS

BRIGHT STARS (coming soon!)

CHILDREN'S SERIES

Get Up, Lil Peter. Get Up!

You Can't Quit, Lil Peter, You Just Can't

Teamwork, Lil Peter, It Works

Pick Me, Lil Peter, Pick Me

Small Things, Lil Peter, Make A Big Difference

Smile Lil Peter, It's A Gift

www.ingramcontent.com/pod-product-compliance
Lightning Source LLC
Chambersburg PA
CBHW030740110726
47900CB00008B/2387